PASSAGES

a collection of short stories and poems

Passages
A Bournemouth Writing Prize anthology
First published 2022 by Fresher Publishing

Fresher Publishing
Bournemouth University
Weymouth House
Fern Barrow
Poole
Dorset BH12 5BB
www.fresherpublishing.co.uk
email escattergood@bournemouth.ac.uk

Cover by: Kimmy Renton, Carolina Marinez
Image: 'Minimal Staircase' by Annie Spratt (2018)

Foreword

Firstly, our small team of would-be editors would like to thank all of those who submitted to The Bournemouth Writing Prize this year. The calibre of work was really high, and we all enjoyed reading your works and going on those journeys with you.

Our group would also like to extend our thanks to all of those involved with the Design, Editing and Publishing Module on the MA Creative Writing and Publishing degree at Bournemouth University, with particular thanks to Emma Scattergood and Fresher Publishing.

The process of selecting, editing and designing this anthology has been an eye-opening, yet fun experience for our group. Whilst not always plain sailing, we feel we have produced an anthology of collective works that encapsulates the mood of our world reawakening from the pandemic. Whilst not explicitly a collection of Covid inspired writing, the need for escape and travel and imagination punches through with every line.

We hope that Passages fills that need for you, as it does us. Happy reading.

Carolina, Chanel, Kimmy & Aramide

Contents

Asylum

By Anna Seidel

Anna Seidel is currently completing her MS in Creative Writing at the University of Oxford alongside a career in economics. She previously read business economics and philosophy at the University of St. Gallen, Switzerland and at Harvard University. Also, she is the co-founder of the poetry foundation 'The Napkin Poetry Review'. Her poetic work has been published in Stanford University's Literature Journal Mantis, Stand, The Fiddlehead, Brittle Star, Inkwell, Marble Poetry, and Frontier Poetry, among others.

Asylum

Crossing my lips, you trace each crest, crease, bend,
the branch jabbed soles of my bifid tongue,
feel thin mountain air sped breath-beats;

Explore raw paths plied in soil, riptides of my mouth,
where prayers of poison, prayers of thorns
near childhood dreams rest;

Where secret thoughts silently take seed,
cradling lost roots on taste buds,
hiding a grief finely sewn into flesh.

Did you find the words that had flout borders,
smuggled in the cavities of my wisdom teeth, tunnels
through which memory haunts my mind
like an endless reverberating tremor?
Did you ever have to measure a word's ballast?

These exiled idioms held so much for so long.
Wrapped in sheepskin, vowels brimming,
their lettered backs broken from all the weight.

In each cavern of a kiss, I search foreign words
to re-sculpt my story from, seek harbor
in strange tongues, that so often fail to hold.

The Little Teapot

By Beth Damms

Beth Damms lives in the French Alps with her husband and cat. She spends most of her time training for triathlon and trail but in her spare time she loves to read and write and draw, inspired by the scenery and nature. Writing has become a real passion and she especially loves the challenge of creating short stories with amusing characters.

The Little Teapot

My body is made of smooth, white porcelain decorated with elegant red and yellow flowers. My lid is blue with a solitary bee flying on the top. Apparently, I have a nice spout and handle, which are also blue. When I was made, there were others, similar in shape but each one different. Someone hand painted different decorations on each of us, I remember it tickled a lot. There was this one teapot that just had small red spots on it, and another with thick blue stripes running around its middle. I think I was one of the luckier ones - I got flowers and a bee. We got put on display in a rustic country barn, and that's when we saw the 'For sale' sign next to us. Bizarrely, we had the same price next to each of us, but the others didn't stand a chance. Of course, I was picked before them. I was the prettiest. A lady saw me and remarked upon my colourful flowers, and I think I remember her saying 'it has a lovely bee on top'. She bought me instantly. I was wrapped in soft tissue paper and boxed. The journey was short and bumpy, but I slept most of the way. When we arrived at her house, she carefully unwrapped me and presented me to her husband.

That's when things started to go wrong...

'We already have a teapot. Why do we need another?' He asked.

'It's just so lovely. It will look nice in the display cabinet,' she replied.

'Hold on! You're not going to use me as an actual teapot? I'm not an ornament... I'm a f****** teapot!' Apparently, she didn't hear me.

I was quickly put on the middle shelf of an ugly cabinet in the corner of the room next to a dancing lady with a shiny dress. And that's where I stayed for countless years.

I had to sit there and watch my owners' boring daily routine, never getting the chance to shine. Occasionally, they had guests and that's when the 'other' teapot came out. It taunted me as it poured out the tea. It was just a mass-made-run of the mill- type teapot you get at the supermarket: plain white with no decoration whatsoever. I felt smug when the guests left and that other teapot returned to the kitchen cupboard. But secretly, I was jealous; at least it was being used for its purpose in life.

Not like me.

I was a 'show teapot'.

The lady was kind to me. She took me out of the stuffy cabinet and dusted me regularly. They were the nice moments. I relished her touch. She would sometimes lift off my lid, and I could imagine hot water being poured into me. Then she would put my lid back on and move on to the figurines. The husband, on the other hand, never even looked at us. But then again, he didn't look at anything other than the television and the porn that he hid behind the cabinet.

I saw many things in that lounge: parties, arguments, randy exchanges on the sofa, but then something new happened. I was the first one to notice the new arrival. It was a baby. A boy. He cried all the time, almost enough to make my glaze crack. I hated him. I named him Poop-Face.

He got bigger and noisier and would sometimes bump into the cabinet. I would wobble a bit and end up askew, annoyingly facing the inside of the cabinet until it was time for my next dusting. I thought to myself, *one day he would knock the cabinet too hard and one of us would fall.*

I was right.

It was a rainy Tuesday. Poop-Face was home playing with his stupid friends. They were chasing each other. 'TAG', they called it. Well, Poop-Face was 'it' and he chased his chubby friend around the sofa. Chubby was slow, and Chubby got 'tagged'. He lost his balance and fell into the cabinet. I've heard them talk about earthquakes on the television and this must have been 7 or 8 on the Richter scale. We all wobbled violently. Poop-Face ran to catch the cabinet from toppling over completely, and we all settled back in our places.

Well, almost all of us did. The shiny dancing lady fell down; the cabinet door swung open, and she fell out onto the hard, wooden floor. Poop-Face knew he was in trouble. The lady ran in when she heard the noise. Poop-Face pointed at Chubby and said, 'it's his fault, he did it.' He was nice like that.

She picked the dancing lady up, examined her, and put her back on the shelf.

'You are lucky she isn't damaged. Go and play outside,' she said calmly.

What! Is that all he gets? Why didn't she give him a good hiding? The husband would have. It could have been a massacre, broken glass and ceramic pieces all over the floor. Our body parts all mixed up like in a mass grave. The dancing lady looked shook up, but she was still smiling, so I guess no harm was done this time.

They talked about having another kid. They tried, but nothing happened. They argued about whose fault it was. They only had one child and they got Poop-Face.

Life is cruel sometimes.

Poop-Face became a teenager. One day his friends were over, and they were bragging about sexual conquests. The chubby one, who was even chubbier now, remembered crashing into the cabinet all those years ago. He thought it was so funny.

'Remember, the whole thing nearly fell down. What

a shame that would have been. All of those ugly things smashed up,' he said sarcastically. 'I wonder what's under her skirt.'

There was nothing I could do.

He opened the cabinet door, took her out with his disgusting fingers and turned her upside down.

'Put her back you bloody pervert!' I yelled.

But when they realised, she was not anatomically correct, they put her back, disinterested.

It wasn't all bad living in the cabinet. Sometimes the television actually had some decent programmes. Sometimes I would see the lady and her husband actually being nice to each other, and I could imagine they were in love once many years ago, before Poop-Face came along and ruined everything. I think I even saw the husband look at me once and smile. It might have been wind. Still, it was a smile.

Poop-Face got older and spent less and less time at home. He looked awful and smelt worse. He constantly made his mum cry and shouted obscenities at his dad. *It's not too late to give him a good hiding*, I thought

One day, Poop-Face walked up to the cabinet, opened the door, and reached in. I am not going to lie, I was terrified. What the HELL was he going to do? He was so angry all the time. He calmly put his grubby hand on my pretty bee lid. *No...I need my lid, please don't smash my lid*. I would rather be completely smashed. A teapot without a lid is useless, it's just a pot. He had his other hand in his pocket and then he took something out of there and put it into my body. I had no idea what it was. He put my lid back on and walked away.

I had strange dreams for days. In one dream, I wasn't a teapot anymore but a teacup. Boiling hot tea cascaded into me, followed by lumps of sugar and creamy milk. Then came a silver spoon and mixed everything together, round and round. It was disorientating and bizarre. In another dream, the bee flew off my lid and came back with more bees. They made a hive in my body using my spout as their entrance. Gooey honey oozed out of me, and the constant buzzing drove me insane.

It turned out Poop-Face had hidden drugs in my body, and I had experienced some of their 'magic'. The lady found them on her next dusting session. That was the biggest argument I ever witnessed. Endless shouting and crying that finally ended with the dad shouting 'Why are you wasting your life like this? I wish we had never had you!'

Poop-Face grabbed the car keys and stormed off.

I never saw him again.

The lady cried every day. The husband tried to comfort her, but she blamed him for what happened and pushed him away. Then, it was the day of the funeral. Close family and friends arrived 'not knowing what to say'. The other teapot was being used to serve the tea. This time, I was happy to be on display.

The lady and the husband stopped talking. Silent meals in front of the TV, no more kisses and cuddles on the sofa, no more happiness. She stopped dusting us altogether. It's amazing how dusty things get, even in a closed cabinet. I could feel a gross, thick, layer of dust on me – I wouldn't have blamed the bee if it did fly off for real this time.

Time went on and several years passed like this. They became old and frail. He died first. The lady seemed a bit happier when she was on her own, but then she started to forget things. At first, little things like where her glasses where, but then she forgot bigger things like turning the gas cooker off. I could smell it. So could her helper, who came to check on her that day.

That's when they took her and put her into a care home.

I don't know who they were, but they came with boxes, lots of boxes, and rolls of bubble wrap. They took the dancing lady first. Layers and layers of bubble wrap enveloped her body until she was just a round blob. Then it was my turn. They wrapped my lid separately and then my body. It was soft in my cocoon, and I felt warm and safe. I don't know how long we spent in that cardboard box, but the day I heard the tape being cut was the happiest day of my life. I was excited to get my lid back on and to see the old lady again.

But it was a man's hand that picked me up. He took a quick look at me and said, 'it's quite decorative, it should sell. I will give you £10.'

'WHAT! You stingy bastard...I am fine porcelain with a unique design...you clearly don't know your teapots.' I yelled.

Why don't they ever hear me?

He was right about one thing though, I did sell.

A woman bought me as a birthday present for her sister. I heard the sister say 'ooh, what could it be? I hope you haven't spent too much on me.' Followed by 'oh, it's a teapot. How nice. Thanks sis.'

Even I could hear the disappointment in her voice. The gift box lid went back on, and I was in darkness again.

When the husband got home from work, I heard muffled voices.

'She bought me a bloody teapot for my birthday! This is because I got her that wrinkle cream. Spiteful cow,' she blurted.

'Well, you do like tea,' he replied.

'I do, but I'm not an old lady who uses a bloody teapot.'

'Maybe she thought it was nice and you would like it.'

'It's bloody ugly and it has a bee on it. She knows I hate bees.'

As you can imagine, I was not a happy teapot. The ungrateful bitch! Ugly? Has she seen her face? She should have kept that wrinkle cream for herself. And what kind of crazy, deranged person hates bees?

The husband suggested she could donate me to charity, and that's where I ended up: back on the shelf—an unwanted present, an unwanted teapot.

It was demoralising.

I wished for someone to at least pick me up so I could feel what it was like to be touched again, or even knock me off the shelf just so my nightmare could be over. I had been a teapot for so long; two owners and never been used as a teapot.

What was the point? My colours had faded, I literally had a chip on my shoulder. I didn't blame anyone for not buying me, I must have looked sad and pathetic.

Customers came and went without buying anything, but then it happened. She was an angel. I'm sure I saw a faint halo around her head when she entered through the door. Her fingers were cold when she touched my porcelain, but I knew straight away her heart was warm.

'You are perfect,' she said sweetly.

PERFECT! No one had ever called me perfect. She paid £10 and put me delicately into her rucksack, like a baby unaware of my surroundings but content with the warmth of my new parent.

Betty was her name. She lived alone, apart from her cat, and talked to herself all the time. She tried to talk to the cat, but he would walk off mid-sentence and turn his back to her – cats can be dicks sometimes. That pissing cat didn't know how lucky he was. She was youngish and attractive in the right light, and I counted five boyfriends in two years. But they didn't last long. She was old-fashioned and wanted commitment and they... well they just wanted sex. I could tell she was lonely. Her job was exhausting, and she changed into her pyjamas as soon as she got home, possibly another reason why her boyfriends didn't last very long.

And Me? I still wasn't being used as a teapot. Betty was 'saving me for best', as she put it. 'Just bloody use me now,' I pleaded, 'I might not have long left, and when is 'best' anyway?'

One evening, she got home from work in a good mood and raised me up lovingly. 'I hope you don't mind, but I am going to take you to work with me tomorrow.'

The cat meowed, demanding his food as he did every night, and she put me back down.

Wait, why am I going to work with you? Are you giving me away?

It was a long night, hundreds of scenarios went through my head, but soon enough it was morning time. She picked me up and carefully put me in her rucksack. I wasn't the only one in there. There was a tin of some sort and a packet of bourbon biscuits. When we arrived at her work, I could smell fustiness with a hint of urine. We went into a room, and I could hear a kettle being boiled. She took the tin out first. Followed by the pack of biscuits.

Then, I heard a familiar voice.

'I wonder if it is the same one...' an old lady said, excitedly.

I was carefully taken out of the bag and put on the table. And there she was. My first owner – Mrs Smith. Older and frailer, but I could still see the twinkle in her eyes.

'It has a bee on it. It's the same one as I used to have. Thank you dear,' Mrs Smith squealed.

Betty smiled. It was the happiest I had ever seen her.

'I will make us some tea. Help yourself to the biscuits,'

Betty said.

This was it. I was finally going to be used as a teapot. It's hard to describe the feeling of that first time. I just hoped my spout would perform! The teabag went in. It was a round one. Tetley, I think. Then the boiling water came pouring inside. I could feel the teabag releasing into the water as they became one. I had a warm feeling as gentle steam released from my spout. It was beautiful. Then, she put one hand on my handle, the other gently on my lid, and tipped me up. Golden, amber liquid poured out of me into the two teacups. It was such a rush. I had dreamt of that moment for so long. But then something weird happened: Betty put me down and put, what I can only describe as a jumper, over me. My spout and handle stuck out of the weird holes. What the hell was happening?

'Get this itchy thing off of me,' I cried, but once I got used to being dressed, it was actually nice. It kept me warm and cosy.

They sat together, drinking tea and chatting about the past. Mrs Smith spoke of her sadness. She said she had many regrets in life – not telling her son she loved him before he died, and not spending more time together as a family. She also mentioned that she wished she had used her favourite teapot instead of putting me on show in the cabinet.

Her final words were 'you have to appreciate people and things when you have them around. Life is for living and loving.'

She fell asleep afterwards.

She didn't wake up, but at least she died happy.

Betty was moved by her time with Mrs Smith and decided to organise a weekly event at the care home for families of the old people to visit and spend quality time with tea and cake. She bought some extra teapots. I admit, some of them were nearly as pretty as me, but I am kept just for Betty. She enjoys the process of making tea at home and has now found someone who she can share her time with. He is old fashioned too and makes her happy. I like him. The only problem is that he's a coffee aficionado. A fancy chrome and glass French press has already moved in next to me in the kitchen.

But we get on and are like one big happy family, and I have finally found my place in life.

Breadcrumbs

By Molly Smith-Main

Molly Smith-Main is an M. A. Creative Writing student at Bournemouth University. She is new to the world of writing stories but loves writing poems. She is particularly interested in reading historical dramas and loves walking along the beach in Bournemouth, especially in the winter.

Breadcrumbs

She looked down at the blank screen with its cursor flashing anxiously in dismay. What did she want to say? 'Help, I'm so lonely!' sounded a little dramatic, and although honest, it didn't seem quite positive enough to make any friends. She scrolled down slowly, pressing the tiny heart-shaped button robotically. Photo after photo of beautifully drawn eyebrows arched over thickly lashed eyes looking away from her and towards some perfect life.

Search #womensfashion

Glancing down at her worn leggings, she unhelpfully smudged a stray speck of tomato soup down her leg. 'What can I say that is going to be even remotely interesting to anybody on here?' She'd had her clothes for ages, and every time she attempted to put on make-up, she ended up looking like a cheap drag artist. Her daughter had been the one who had suggested she create an Instagram account. Pearl posted a photo every day and said it would be a lovely way of seeing what the grandchildren were up to. It had taken her a while to get used to it – all these buttons and scrolling were slightly different from the typewriter she had learned on at school, but now she had the hang of it; she loved seeing their smiling faces and what they had been up to. She wished she could see more of them, but they lived so far away.

Search #missinggrandchildren

She frowned as she scrolled past a photo of a bowl of food, broccoli and sweetcorn, something black and some rice. She was still completely confused about why people thought it was remarkable that they had made some food. She tried to imagine collecting a fat packet of photographs from Boots, after anxiously waiting for a few days, only to be greeted by plates of beans on toast, bowls of cornflakes and a mug of tea.

Search #whydopeoplepostpicturesoffood?

Pearl had thought Instagram might help her make friends – friends in her phone as she called them – as she didn't get out much anymore, especially now. She had only spoken face to face with one person this week, and that was Will at the paper shop when she had run out of teabags. She couldn't remember when she'd become so isolated and introverted? Perhaps when she had left the factory four years ago after over 30 years of service – she missed her colleagues there, missed their chats in the tea-room and the feeling of camaraderie as they put on their aprons and hairnets and trooped into the 'oven' as they called it. Dr Jacob had suggested she 'get out more'. But where was she to go?

Search #getoutmore

It was 11.00 am, time for her morning mug of tea. This Instagram could take up the whole morning if she let it. She sat at her kitchen table, looking out the window at the trees at the bottom of her garden. Her Dad had planted that apple tree before her elder brothers and her were born. They had loved eating the apples and climbing in the branches if their mum wasn't looking.

After lunch finished at 1.00 pm sharp, she put on the radio, pulled her apron over her head, and began making her bread. She had always loved the smell of fresh bread ever since her father had come home from the bakery with a warm white loaf wrapped in crunchy brown paper. Her mum had coarsely sliced the loaf, and they would all sit around the kitchen table stuffing chunks of soft bread dripping with melting margarine into their hungry mouths. She tipped out the mix and began to push and fold, squash, and knead the warm, pliable dough. As she squished, she thought back to when her daughter was little, how she had played happily in the street, laughing loudly and crying for attention when she had fallen over or was hungry. She'd had to work hard at the time, juggling work and family but never realised just how lucky she was to have all her loved ones around her. She had adored being a mum, keeping her baby safe and warm, listening to her read and encouraging Pearl to keep learning. She had told her stories every night before bedtime. One of their favourite stories was Hansel and Gretel. She'd always thought Hansel was so clever to leave a little trail of breadcrumbs so they could find the way back. She smiled when she remembered her daughters' squeals of delight as she read about the witch in her cottage in the woods. She wondered now if the witch was just a lonely, old woman. Stuck in her house looking out at the trees, pleased for some young company and smiling faces.

Search #lonelywomen

Well, blimey, that was a search she wasn't going to try again.

She'd been ever so proud when her daughter had gone to university. She was the first person from the family to go, and her degree had meant she had been able to get a good job – it was just a shame she had moved so far away as she'd have loved to be able to help to look after the kids.

Search #grandma

Since she was no longer working, she had sorted through all her clothes and washed and mended the ones she wore. She scrolled once again through photos of glossy haired women, teeth so white they almost looked blue, wearing tiny, figure-hugging dresses and huge, towering heels clutching branded patent bags and enormous sunglasses as they jetted off to some exotic, luxury holiday. She'd been on holiday a few times but never left England. Her late husband hadn't wanted to travel, but they had saved up and

gone to Bournemouth a few times. She had loved the feel
of the sun and sand on her skin. They had stayed in a B&B
looking over Boscombe Pier, somehow fish and chips tasted
even better at the seaside. It had been three years now since
he had gone. The house was too quiet without him.

Search #matureladiesfashion

Ah, that was a bit more like it – there were pictures
of 'real' people, wearing 'normal' clothes. Also, a few
interesting posts about women her age. Silver-haired ladies.
Even a post about 'empowering women'. She wondered
if she had ever been empowered. The famous Bread
Shortages of 1977? She had stood outside the factory with
her pal, Sue and all their workmates, waving their placards,
striking for extra money. Sue had died last winter after
suffering from throat cancer. They had all felt powerful
when they returned to work and were given a few pounds
extra in their wage packet. Felt rather daring now.

As she walked through the hall, she caught a glimpse of
herself in the mirror. Her hair was a yellowing grey as she
neared her 70th year. She had kept it long and usually wore
it tied in a ponytail, just as she had when she was younger
and had to keep it tucked in a net cap for the factory. The
radio was playing a song by The Beatles, and she suddenly
felt like a teenager again. She carefully hauled the loaf out
of the oven and set it on a cooling rack. It was a thing of
beauty. The golden crust glistened in the light from the
window, and the smell was amazing. She decided to take
a photo of it and send it to Pearl. The grandchildren had
always loved her bread too. After a few attempts – one of
which involved her getting a rather disturbing photo of
herself with what looked like a huge chin – she got one she
was happy with and sent it off to Pearl.

'Wow! Mum, that looks like a delicious loaf!! Jack and
Meg would love some of that! I'll post it on your Instagram

page! #artisanbread – Take care, see you soon! P xxx'

The next morning, she switched her phone on. A little red circle was on her Instagram button. When she clicked on it, she saw the photo of her bread had over 836 likes. There were so many comments and questions, too –

This looks amazing!

How did you make this?

I wish I could do that!

Can I help the recipe?

You've inspired me to bake bread!

How did you get the crust so golden? Mie never looks like that!

And 127 people wanted to follow her – whatever that meant.

Heat-Stroke

By Chloe Moorehouse

Chloe Moorehouse is a 23-year-old student at Bournemouth University studying English. From a young age, she has always had a passion for writing. When she was 6 years old, she, alongside five other students, wrote and published a book, Fox Learns a Lesson. Currently, she is working towards writing a young adult's fiction novel as part of her university dissertation.

Heat-Stroke

What happens when you die? Studies show that visual or auditory hallucinations are often part of the dying experience.

I pushed my glasses up onto my face and continued reading.

The lack of oxygen impacts the temporal lobe and causes a chemical imbalance in the brain.

I leaned back in my chair and stared at the curtains. Taking off my glasses, I began to massage the bridge of my nose.

My God this is dull, I thought. *Is it too late to change courses?*

I leaned over to grab my lighter with a sigh, and relit the dying flame from my candle. Flipping the page of my notebook, I was ready to delve back in.

My phone buzzed. Rachel had sent me another dog video. I swivelled on my chair and opened the link. My thumb habitually went to scroll on to watch more.

No. I scolded myself. *You need to get this done for tomorrow.*

Locking my phone, I turned back in my chair to face the desk and was greeted by a scorching blaze.

Holy Shit!

I had flipped my notepad page onto the candle flame. Watching my research disintegrate into the flickering abyss, I was struck with fear. I shot up. I grabbed my cup of water, panicked, and threw it onto the fire. Stamping out the remaining embers with my palms, I managed to finally put out.

I could still feel the heat from the fire on my hands. Still smell the burning paper in my nose. I went into the

bathroom to hold them under the water. The cool flow
eased both the pain and the shaking. I splashed a few drops
onto my face and leaned my hands on the basin. I looked
up into the mirror at the shaky mess before me.

Calm down, I told myself. *It's over now. You're fine.*

I inspected my hands for damage and noticed a few red
marks on my right palm.

Nothing to worry about. It could have been a lot worse.

I cleared my throat to relieve my achy chest.

Walking back into my room, my heart rate had finally
started to slow. The nervous sweatiness of my palms had
almost soothed them. I glanced down at my desk and
saw the charred remains of my revision. I picked up my
bedroom bin and scooped all the blackened bits of paper
into it.

That's me up all night now redoing those notes.

Grabbing a make-up wipe from my bedside table, I swept
it across the surface until the only evidence of the fire was
the slight burning smell in the air. I reached over the desk
to open the window and let some fresh air in. My fingers
touched the scalding hot handle.

I snatched my hand back from the handle. Shaking it
in the air and rubbing it on my trousers to ease the pain. I
pulled my left hand up to examine it. Bracing myself for the
damage, I looked down.

What?

Not an injury in sight.

Confused, I gingerly leaned back towards the window
frame and touched the handle with my index finger. Stone
cold.

Maybe my hand was still hot from stamping out the fire,
I told myself. *Either that or it was the heat of this room.*

With the adrenaline now gone from my body, I was left
with an aching hand and a realisation of how hot the house

actually was. Unbearably hot even.

I pulled off my hoodie and walked towards the thermostat in the living room.

17.5. Surely not. It must be broken again.

I turned the dial down even so. On the way back to my room, I stopped at the kitchen to fill a glass of water from the tap. That's when I heard three sharp bangs. I turned my head towards the hallway.

Who on earth could that be at this time of night?

Walking towards the front door, I peered through the glass panels. I could see my car and the bushes but no person. No one was there. No logical culprit of the banging. My hand reached up and held the chain, debating whether to open the door and have a proper look.

My common sense got the better of me.

It's probably not the best idea to be outside at this time of night.

I slid the chain back onto the latch.

I left the door open to cool the room down, put my glass of water onto the bedside table, picked up the textbook and sat down onto the bed to try the text again.

With only snippets of reality breaking through, these hallucinations can be so vivid the dying person may not even realise what is happening.

My reading was cut short by another loud thud. This time, the sound came from the back door of the house.

For Christ's sake, what is that now?

The book dropped onto my pillow as I headed back out into the corridor to investigate. Walking in the direction of the sound, I turned my head momentarily towards the front door.

Definitely no one there, I told myself. *Although I must remember to put the latch on the door before I go to bed.*

Wait.

The latch.

I stopped in my tracks and turned around. Staring at the front door, I thought back.

I put it on. I definitely put the latch on.

I reached and connected the link to the metal slit. The shaking of my hand caused the chain to rattle. This noise, combined with the ringing in my ears, almost made me miss the sounds going on around me. Until I heard it again. Two soft footsteps. From right next to me.

I ran.

Ran back to my room as fast as I could and slammed the door shut. Sliding down the smooth wooden surface to the rough carpet beneath me, I put my head in my hands. My heart was beating so hard, so fast that I could swear I saw it beneath my top. All the heat in my body rushed down towards my sweaty palms. I felt the warm air push shakily out of my nostrils onto my top lip. I dared not to breathe out of my mouth to alert whoever or whatever it was outside the room of my location.

There I sat, waiting. For something, anything to happen. I filled my lungs with air and tried to slow my pulse down. The logical part of my brain kicked in.

If there was something out there, it would have tried to get in by now.

Slowly, I bared my weight onto my quivering legs and stood back up. I backed up from the door and paused again. Nothing. I could only hear the sound of my beating heart and the soft hum of the lightbulb. I wasn't totally reassured. I could still see the goosebumps on my arms and feel the fear coursing through my veins.

I walked the few short steps until I reached the foot of the bed. Thankfully, my phone was right there on top of the duvet. I unlocked it and selected my phonebook. I pressed the green button and held it up to my ear. Hearing the dialling tone, I pleaded with myself for her to answer. When I heard a crackle, I looked down at the screen and saw the phone call had been answered.

'Mum?'

The crackling continued. I spoke anyway.

'Mum? I think there's someone in the house.'

I paused to wait for her reply.

The crackling was interrupted by her shouting down the phone: 'Where is she? Where is she?'

'What? I don't even know if it is a girl. What are you talking about?'

'Jess! Oh my God, Jess!' I could hear the panic in my mum's voice. I heard her crying. Then the phone cut out.

What had just happened? I tried redialling, but the screen remained black. Quickly, I reached down to plug it into the charger. I saw movement in the corner of my eye. Dropping my phone, I spun around. That's when I saw that my bedroom door was wide open, and something was blocking the light from the hallway: a dark figure; shiny and covered in a warm, orange glow. Coming towards me.

No.

No.

I backed up against the wall of my bedroom. My heart was in such a panic, I could no longer hear it beating. I could feel nothing but the sharp pain in my chest. Feel it tearing through my body. Splitting me in half.

I couldn't breathe.

I couldn't-

I opened my eyes to a blinding white light. The brightness engulfed me. As I blinked my eyes into focus, the glow that consumed my vision shrunk to six lit up tiles above my head. I focused my attention on the dust particles in the air. From my left, I heard a faint beeping. I tried to turn my head towards the noise, but it wouldn't move. Only my eyes could follow the sound.

Straining, I turned my eyes as far as they could go until I saw a multitude of clear tubes coming down from above me. I saw a large, grey machine that seemed to be the source of the steady beeping. My body throbbed at this effort.

Looking down, I saw that my arms and legs were covered in pristine, white bandages.

What the hell happened to me?

I focused back on the particles in the bright light above me and tried to take a deep breath in, feeling with full force the tube down my throat. I began choking. Spluttering. With my body's most natural instinct being unable to do its job. My burning throat began to heave. The pain of my lungs soared through my chest. The beeping was no longer steady, resembling more of an alarm sound. The room was suddenly occupied with a woman.

'Jess. Calm down you're okay.'

The woman in front of me was a stranger, wearing a dark blue outfit and a face mask. She took a tentative step towards me and reached out to touch my arm with her gloved hand.

'You're okay,' she said again. 'Focus on me. Listen to what I'm saying.'

I stared at her, and the beeping slowed back down.

'Don't fight it. The tube is keeping you alive. Do you know where you are? Your ventilator is stopping you from speaking right now, but can you nod or shake your head?'

I was unable to move my head to give her an answer.

'That's okay. You have received a large number of sedatives that your muscles may not have broken down yet. You're in St. John's hospital. You've been in a fire, Jess. You were quite badly hurt.'

A fire? What fire?

'My name is Dr. Thompson. You may feel a bit stiff. You've been unconscious for a few days.'

A few days? I was in my room moments ago.

'I'm afraid you have suffered some quite serious injuries. You have third-degree burns covering seventy percent of your body. When the paramedics brought you in, you had suffered acute respiratory syndrome, which unfortunately led to respiratory failure.'

What? I don't understand.

'Your heart stopped, Jess. For several minutes. We did electrical cardioversion and thankfully brought you back.'

My heart stopped? I died?

'Your mum's in the waiting room. She's been here from the moment you were brought in. I just need to check you over, and then you can see her.'

My mum? I was just on the phone to her.

She walked over to the machine that was pushing the air inside my chest and pressed a few buttons. My eyes scanned the room around me; the white walls, the machines, the equipment around me, and the smell of sanitiser in the air. I tried to process what she was telling me.

I was in a fire? I died?

The beeping from my left sped up.

But I put the fire out.

The candle fire. I put it out.

I put it out.

Didn't I?

The Road Back

By Sandra

Sandra is new to writing and is very excited about it. She has been writing match reports and social news for my local golf club. She retired from teaching Communications in University College Cork.

The Road Back

Twelve steps to freedom
Or maybe it's not
what we can expect in this changing of ways.
Step by careful step, life evolves
not as it was but as it's resolved to be.

Who is this new person inhabiting our space?
Why does she have my mammy's face?
Words remembered with searing effect
Once dismissed, now proud of place
In a world of re-learning and maternal embrace.

Too late? Why now? It is time for release of guilt
 and of shame and of blame to replace
with new life, new living, new people of worth
including the writer who's entrenched in his hurt.

Live and let live is the cant of the group of all sorts
of revivors and experts who
advise, and chastise and hasten to add
One day at a time and take care of your head.

Thirteen in a room, each taking a slot
To explain how it works, how it is,
how it's got to this stage of despair where all dignity's lost,
and it's time for release from the chains of the past.
All working together to claim a result, to search
and re-live and construct a new plan
to replace one that's broken or falling apart.

There's Martha, whose children have cut themselves off and
Philip whose search for a life full of love is
hampered and hindered and has taken a drop 'til
he wonders if the journey is likely to stop.

Mick the abuser who learned all he knew from the uncle
whose love sent his values askew
and Anna whose gripe lay with drink and the like
is struggling with concepts beyond her true psyche.

Where will it end? And where will we go?
Where there's hope to find out the true self in the know
Where mindsets are clear and the brain's battleground
falls away in the peace that can always be found
In love and in knowledge that always was there
tho' hidden quite deeply by fog and by fear
of finding out truly what was never laid bare,
in our youth, in our prime,
In the passage of time.

From Tenerife With Love

By Aby Atilol

Aby Atilol is a product manager by day. Somehow in her busy schedule she finds time to write short stories. She recently completed an online short story course at City Lit.UK and is more interested in the short story form than ever before.

From Tenerife With Love

The hair that once ran past her shoulders, the envy of all the girls in her age group, lies in a clay pot in the corner of the room. Chiamanda had lost count of the number of times Ada had nicked her scalp with the blade.

'Bring it nearer,' Ada motions to the young girl holding the lamp. Another girl surveys the mud floor and picks up the hair that falls like the dark clouds at their feet.

'I still can't see,' Ada says, tilting Chiamanda's head up and down.

'Tomorrow, we do the rest.'

Ada lets her breath out, she had been holding it all through the cutting, as if breathing would slow her down. She hands Chiamanda a tub of coconut oil and a piece of the mirror she had tucked into her wrapper.

'*Ndo* – sorry, my sister. You know this is the way of our people. Your husband's death is a shock to the whole village, may his soul rest in peace.'

She takes a step back, hands on hips, satisfaction with a job well done visible on her face. Chiamanda rubs her hand over her scalp wincing at the million and one cuts on her head. They could have done this at day break.

The tradition that dictates every aspect of life in the Niger Delta demands that a woman's hair be shorn when her husband dies. Chiamanda wonders if this is to make the widow less attractive, to shame her or to take something else away from her. As if losing your husband in his prime is not the ultimate dethronement of a married woman.

'Are you really going to shave my armpits and the hair down below?' she asks. 'How does that appease the gods? What do the gods do with my hair? Do they burn it as some dumb offering?' From the looks on their faces, Chiamanda knows she has said a little too much.

It was difficult not to question the ways of her people when she was learning new ways of being from the pale skinned visitors. They had arrived long before her grandparents were born and before their parents. They showed no sign of leaving, when one group got old and tired or fever got the better of them, another group arrived.

'Remember our ways are what sets us apart from the visitors,' her mother said when she decided to stop wearing her *Adala*. She'd been wearing the brass anklets since she had come of age. Growing up meant wearing the ridiculous circles of brass around each ankle. Walking was a nightmare as each leg had to swing wide and clear of the other to avoid tripping over.

To people of the Niger Delta, tradition is everything: it dictates what you eat, and your position in life. It governs when you come of age, and when you do, the caste you can marry from and what happens when that union ends.

Coming of age meant she could no longer wrestle with the boys in her age group, climb trees for the fun of climbing, and she had to get married. That bit she didn't mind, as her husband, Nduka, was a great catch. He spoke the visitors' language and knew their ways. His hard work on the farm meant she, and the two sons she bore him, never went hungry. She taught him all that her mother had passed onto her. How to source and make potions for the *fluenza*, and how to cure a fever with lemongrass and bark from the Cinchona tree.

As a boy he had been sent to school to make up the numbers. None of the other chiefs would send their children. 'Why learn another man's language and customs when our customs serve us well?' they said. And so Nduka and others like him – born of slave women and free men – learnt to read and write before the free born.

Nduka was chosen to be the 'ears' of the king of Opobo, the centre of palm oil production in the delta. King Jaja liked his humility and his ability to switch from his native Igbo to the harsh sounding vowels of the English and German visitors.

The visitors never come into the village unannounced. On the day they brought the news, their runners came panting into the square like pregnant dogs. Their Khaki shirts dripping with sweat and the fine red sand that announced the arrival of the harmattan season. On that day, the curlews began their calls before sundown causing everyone to pause and look at each other with an unspoken question. What are the gods angry about now? Even the dogs that lazed around for most of the day stood with their ears upright as if they could hear something inaudible to everyone else.

Four months earlier, the visitors had announced that King Jaja had been released from exile in Jamaica. They had been tricked onto the ship that took them to Jamaica. The latest was that the king and his manservant Nduka had died in Tenerife on the last leg of their journey home.

Before she can run, Chiamanda is banished to the store room in her compound. Thirty days of confinement begin without warning. Her mother looks on helplessly as the *Umunna* – older womenfolk surround her like mother hens, telling her what she can and cannot do. Delighting in her terror and their misplaced importance.

At sunrise, a young girl she'd 'bought' from a middleman a few days back brings her food. Two pieces of cocoyam, a pinch of salt, and red palm oil. Crisscross blisters cover the girl's back. Her skin is the colour of the pale kola nuts.

Chiamanda had found them hiding in the bush; a chain securing the girl to the man, waiting for sunrise to continue their journey to the place where the River Niger meets the big sea.

'Eight British pounds,' said the man when she asked him to let her go. She offered him five pounds and eighty manilas.

'No-one uses manilas,' he said when she handed them over, throwing them in the dirt as if they were worthless. Paper money has replaced manilas.

'Take it or I report you to the visitor-in-charge.'

He'd picked up the c-shaped iron rings and scurried off back into the bush.

The people of the Opobo say they have stopped the trade, but every war seems to bring people they cannot feed. People with facial scars that should tell them where they come from. People with the same skin colour, whose language their hosts cannot understand. The prisoners of war become slaves and are put to work harvesting the palm fruit for the king and the supercargoes. The supercargoes are the most disliked visitors. They strut about the village, boasting about the money they'll make for their employers in far off places. When the harvest is over, or there are more workers than work, they sell the workers to supercargoes from Cameroon in exchange for British pounds. For material they call Indian madras. For imported gin that makes grown men sleep all day; ignore their crops and do stupid things. And for heavy velvet material soft and redundant in the hot and clammy Niger delta.

After two nights in confinement, Ada and one of the slave girls lead Chiamanda to the stream on the outskirts of the village. Custom demands she bathes at night in waters away from the village. Her friends follow a few paces behind wielding cutlasses and singing praise songs for Nduka.

'Will you shut up,' shouts Chiamanda.

'No amount of praise singing and god pleasing will

change what has happened.'

They walk back in silence, her friends watching for night creatures and sleep walking supercargoes.

Chiamanda spends the night in the food store with the mice and the stars for company, a broken piece of mirror ready if required. She is awake before the first slither of light breaks the horizon. It's a time when children are in deep sleep and husband and wives, satiated with the activities of the night, lay splayed like pigs roasting on spits. Even the crickets and the owls are silent. Lone hyenas cackle in the distance, searching for food, a mate or anything to keep them busy before sunup. She watches night turn to day. She can make out the shapes of hunters with their quivers of poisoned arrows, antidotes in small gourds around their waist. Their knives are sharp and holstered. The leather amulets around their biceps hide magic potions said to make them invisible. If she can see them, surely others can too. They move like shadows, merging into one another, noiseless footsteps sure on the ground.

As a curious child, she once followed a group deep into the forest. She watched as the bramble yielded to their cutlasses like warm fingers through shea butter. She watched them scale trees and collect honey without being stung. She saw grass snakes dive for cover, and tree monkeys hide their young. They led her round in circles until she came face to face with a wall of bare-chested men.

'Who saw you?' shouted the tallest, his morning breath almost knocking her over.

'It's an abomination for a woman to hunt with men.'

'No-one. I couldn't sleep,' she said.

Nduka, then a 15-year-old strapping lad, pointed out that she was not yet a woman. They let her go. She managed to evade slavers and hunters by following the same path back.

She followed the honeyguide birds that fed on the wax in the bee's nests on the outskirts of the village. She slept underneath piles of leaves between the buttress roots of Iroko trees. She counted two sunsets; she was home before the third.

The visitor-in-charge holds court in the village square. He says they died in Tenerife. Someone put poison in their tea. 'Why poison them now?' ask the people. The orderlies stand to attention, sweating like trussed up pigs, batons at the ready, one eye on their people the other on the visitor-in-charge. From her confinement, Chiamanda can hear the questions fired at the visitor-in-charge:

'Where is this Tenerife place?' they ask.

'Was he not a protected British citizen?'

'How come the governor-general let our king die?'

'They did five years in exile, only to die on the way home.'

'Why were they drinking tea? Is Tenerife cold?'

'Where are their bodies? We must bury our king. If there is no body, there is no palm oil.'

'He must have known the end was near,' she says to the ants marching across the hard mud floor of the store. He knew how to use the beautiful deadly flowers. He would have known when the time was right. They say the sun shines in Jamaica and people of their colour work the land, while visitor people parade like peacocks. They say stolen people from Bonny, Opobo, and people from where the River Niger meets the big sea can be found in this place. They speak the language of the visitors. If they survived five years in a place like that, then why?

The dogs have gone back to lifting their heads only to avoid being stepped on and wagging their tails when the flies become bothersome. The cuts on her scalp have scabbed over, and the hairs the blade missed are rough against her palm. Her stomach complains and readies itself as the heady aromas of roasting goat meat waft through the village. The meat will not touch her lips as it is taboo for a widow to eat food cooked for the funeral of her husband. Crying is forbidden as her husband was a titled man. The night hides her tears and listens to her questions. Her husband did not die in a war. He was not captured and sold like many before him. There is no body to wash and prepare for the journey back home. To ancestors that did not protect him or the King. She is spared the indignity of sitting with his body, fanning flies and watching a once mighty man rot into nothingness. A man at home with his people and with visitors that do not leave.

The vats used to boil the palm fruit are quiet, the slaves slip away at night. The supercargoes get tetchy. Their employers expect their palm oil consignment and a handsome profit. They pass the time making half-visitor babies, fighting fevers and supping over-fermented palm wine.

On the twentieth day of confinement, the wife of the visitor-in charge visits the village with the twin-girl she adopted. Her long skirt swishes the dust as she walks. She weighs the new-born babies and writes things in her book. She wraps strips of white material around the remains of their umbilical cords. These babies will have belly buttons that stay on the inside. The twin girl sticks to the wife of the visitor-in charge like a shadow. To her people, the Efik and Kalabari, twins are bad luck. They leave them in the forest to perish or be rescued by the visitors that do not believe in the evil of an innocent newborn. Her face bears the scars of inquisitive animals that must have wondered if she would be better off as food.

The girl and the wife of the visitor-in-charge check on Chiamanda. A fine film of harmattan dust covers their clothes. Their lips are cracked like everyone else's. The woman talks slowly, the girl translates. The visitor's wife takes Chiamanda hands into hers and prays like the visitors do. To a God they cannot see, a God they say has a son and is everywhere. A God that does not demand offerings. As she prays, she passes Chiamanda a small brass tobacco box. The box is decorated with Palm trees and coconuts made from mother of pearl. It is marked Tenerife, 1891.

In the box are remnants of dried flowers, dried berries and odd shaped seeds. She knows he must have had a good reason to do it and that she cannot tell anyone. She knows that, one day, the visitors will leave. She knows where to find the flowers and seeds to restock the box. She knows that, one day, her children or her children's children will go to Tenerife, find where they buried him and bring him home.

Chiamanda's twenty-eighth day in confinement comes and goes. The *Umunna* and her in-laws are no longer interested in her. Her scalp is covered with soft fuzzy brown hair. Her age group friends visit and gossip. Her children are well, they tell her. Her once smooth mahogany skin, admired by the village menfolk, is dry and grey; falling like fish scales as she moves.

She dreams of festivals and dances gone by. Of running away. Of picking the good bits from the visitors' way of life and weaving them into her own. Of places far away where, according to the wife of the visitor-in-charge, solid water falls from the sky. Of places where people cover themselves with layers of soft, heavy velvet.

Calico

By Everett Jay Buchanan

Everett is a third-year scriptwriting student at Bournemouth University. He is Bulgarian and grew up in the country's capital, Sofia. Everett started writing when he was ten years old and dreamt of being a novelist, albeit that he's directed those ambitions at being a screenwriter instead. He often draws inspiration from popular media and music. Everett does drag in his free time and is often informed by this in his writing.

Calico

I met a woman from an ancient land
Hair disheveled and covered in beige powder
Skin as black as the winter sky,
eyes narrowed and full of armed tragedy.
A skull under her hand,
she runs through the desert.

Half covered visage laid bare to be covered
Pretty flowers but not for her
Wrinkled lips from singing at the sky, a passion read in her
posture
There she stood, a queen amongst eagles
Cacti raising, a sole pole stretched and eroded from the
ground.
A boundless sky above
The finite horizon stretches.

The pole pierces the head,
A white creature with antennae
like an alien stretching out.
A hollow mind,
empty to rot and judgemental destitute eyes
Lips bound by a calico
a rose with a bow flying like a kiss into the lonely summer
air.

We stand alone
Me and her.
Her and the head.
Adorning the grave with the flowers she wishes to have
I stand there too
wishing for a kiss by the same calico.
The queen of knights and her desolate kingdom,
An idol amongst tangerine skies and nights marked with a
hundred stars
An idol amongst the vast cape of red dust that will soon
bleed through the ossein.

Home Home

By Niamh Donnellan

Niamh Donnellan is a writer from Meath, Ireland. Working in communications, she shares other people's stories for a living. Outside office hours, she writes her own. She won the Anthology Short Story Competition 2020 and was selected for the XBorders 2019 and 2020 projects with the Irish Writers Centre. As well as writing a novel, she is currently finishing her first collection of short stories and dabbling in poetry.

Home Home

Ciara could feel spring in the air as she drove home. The fields by the motorway unspooled a flickering tape of lambs playing on fresh green grass, cattle raising their heads to the sky after a long winter indoors, and juddering tractors ploughing the waking earth. Luke snored gently in his car seat, lulled to sleep by the sound of the radio and the warm sun. Ciara's phone rang and she tapped the dashboard quickly so as not to wake him. Her sister's voice came through, breathless.

'Where are you?'

'Nearly home. I'm going to do a spring clean.'

'Great, I'll call over in twenty minutes, I'm out for a walk.'

'No, not Dublin. I meant home home.'

'Offaly? You drove all the way there this morning?'

'Yes. Someone needs to keep an eye on the place.'

'Someone needs to sell the place. It's been two years.'

'Someone.'

'Yeah. Someone.'

She could hear her sister smile.

'Fine. Enjoy the day out. Say hello to the old place for me.'

'Will do.'

Two years, had it really been that long? Ever since her mother died, their family home had lain empty. At first the freshness of grief stopped them from thinking about what to do next. When her brother finally broached the subject the following Christmas, gently suggesting that they sell the house and split the profit, she surprised herself with the strength of her reaction. No. It was still too soon. How about keeping it as a summer home for the three families?

Somewhere to create happy childhood memories for the next generation. The others had scrunched up their faces. The house was a 1970's bungalow in the middle of nowhere, not a picturesque seaside cottage. Dragging the kids there had been hard enough when it involved a visit to Granny and Grandad. Without them, it was just a cold, dark building with no internet. But it was Christmas Day, they'd all had a few drinks, best to leave it.

Another year went by. The house remained empty and her dreams of sunny family holidays hadn't come to pass. Her brother was in Australia and her sister had never found the time. To be fair, her own family weren't overly keen either. The first time they went down was Easter and the kids complained of the cold. So they waited until the height of summer to go again and were eaten alive by midges. The following year John had insisted on two weeks in France. Then it was Autumn, back to school and the weekend routines of football matches and swimming lessons, Halloween parties, snowy December roads, icy January roads, St. Patrick's Day parades, and before she knew it, the days were getting longer again and nobody had been down home in months.

She turned left onto the familiar road past a copse of trees at the edge of their field, and then the old house was in sight. There it was, unchanged, sitting back from the road down a narrow potholed lane lined with nodding daffodils. The hedgerows were alive with little songbirds who flew and perched, flew and perched, just ahead of the car as if leading her on. Smoke curled out lazily from the chimney.

It took her a minute to register the activity. Weird. She'd just spoken to her sister, who else could be there? Maybe a neighbour had come to check the place? Paddy down the road was well known for taking matters into his own hands.

Mam had been convinced he had binoculars to watch the comings and goings of the neighbours. She would bet money he still had a spare key for 'emergencies', the word having quite a loose definition in his books. She pulled up to the house and hopped out of the car. Bloody cheek of the man. She hauled a sleepy Luke from his car seat and marched up to the back door. Just as she suspected, it wasn't locked. She flung it open.

A man stood bent over the kitchen table, his back to her. Not Paddy. This man was around her age, dark hair, dark skin. Ciara let out a scream at the intruder. The man turned around at the unexpected sound, revealing a small girl around Luke's age sitting at the table, drawing with crayons. The little girl looked up at Ciara with big brown eyes, assessed the threat as minimal and went back to her drawing. Ciara frowned. This didn't look like a burglary.

'What are you doing here?'

The man looked more worried than aggressive.

'I live here.'

'No you don't. This is my house.'

'You are Maureen?'

'No. That's my mother. Was my mother. It's my mother's house. My family home. How do you know Mam?'

'There is still some post coming. I keep it there.'

He pointed to a neat pile of letters and leaflets on the counter.

'So, who are you? A squatter?'

'I am Abdullah. This is my daughter Lena. I am sorry, my English, squatter?'

'Oh for Christ's sake. You are here without permission ... illegally ... not allowed ... criminal..."

'Yes. I apologise.' He bowed his head.

'Right. Well. That's not good enough.'

'Yes, of course.'

They stood in silence. A loud snap made Ciara jump. The toaster had popped. Lena tugged on her father's sleeve. Abdullah shrugged at Ciara in the universal language of 'kids, what can you do?' Ciara watched as he buttered the toast and cut it into little triangles before placing the plate in front of his daughter. Luke took the chance to wiggle out of her arms. He climbed onto a chair and began eating the toast alongside Lena. Ciara felt her head start to spin and, stumbling slightly, she sat down heavily on Dad's armchair by the stove.

Abdullah looked concerned.

'Can I offer you tea? For the shock?'

'Em, yes ok.'

He filled the kettle and took two mugs from the draining board, spoons from the drawer and tea bags from the press. It was the practised routine of a man at home in his own kitchen. It set her teeth on edge. He handed her a mug of pale, yellow liquid.

'It's zouhourat, made from hibiscus flowers, calming.'

She took a small sip. It tasted sweet and flowery. The warm sound of daytime radio chatted in the background. Abdullah sat at the kitchen table staring at the mug of tea in front of him.

She felt the blood return to her face and her anger flared again in the face of his serenity.

'So why did you think it was ok to break into somebody else's home?'

He leaned forward slightly and began to speak.

'I came to Ireland from Syria three years ago. We decided to leave when my wife became pregnant. A fresh start, you know. We reached a refugee camp in Turkey. Unfortunately ...'

He glanced at Lena.

'Unfortunately, my wife did not survive the birth.'

He gulped down some tea.

'I continued on to Ireland. I was told that we would be placed temporarily in a direct provision centre while my application was processed. But it is taking much longer than I expected. I cannot work until my case is heard. I thought why not improve my English, so I volunteered at a charity shop a few days a week. A nice Nigerian lady looked after Lena while I worked. I took the bus to Tullamore and that is when this all began.'

'When what began?' Ciara asked impatiently. She hadn't asked for his life story, no matter how harrowing.

'I stared out the bus window for two months at this empty house. I imagined living here, Lena playing in the garden. Finally, one day I got off the bus and walked down the lane, looking in the windows at the dusty rooms. I waited one more month. I did not want to be this person who steals a home, a squinter?'

'Squatter.'

'Yes, I did not want to be this person, so I waited and dreamed. But I decided on Lena's third birthday I could not face another year of my little bird living in a cage. My friend has a phrase: "better to ask forgiveness than permission".'

Ciara huffed.

'So, I packed our bags, and we took the bus in the rain to the house. Oh, Lena thought it was such an adventure.'

He smiled at Ciara as a fellow parent and then seemed to catch himself. He sat up straighter.

'I never took it for granted, I assure you. I made repairs, worked in the garden, planted vegetables.' He tapped the table to bullet point his productivity. 'I have a list of work I will do around the house.'

He pointed to the fridge where there was indeed a long list pinned amongst Lena's crayon drawings.

'I am truly sorry. For me, I would stay in direct provision, but for Lena ... I had to take this chance. Even these few months have been good for her. To play in the garden. To have her own room. I would like to stay here in *sha allah,* God willing. Maybe we could make an arrangement ... but I understand this is your home. I have no right.'

With that he trailed off. His face that had become animated lapsed back into resignation as he waited for another nameless Irish person to decide his fate.

Ciara's breathing had slowed as he talked. At first, she barely heard what he said, anger drumming in her ears. But gradually his quiet voice and the warm kitchen took their effect. She looked around. He had kept the place well - even, truth be told, improved upon it. The kitchen was neat as a pin. The sink was polished to a high sheen and it looked like he had repaired the leaky tap. There was a vase of flowers on the windowsill, daffodils from the garden mixed with some greenery from the hedge. Mam always did it that way too. She hadn't seen the house this clean and cosy in years. His story too sounded plausible. It chimed with all those news articles and opinion pieces in the papers lamenting the fate of asylum seekers in Ireland. She had read them in sympathy and indignation and had signed the petitions.

She paused before speaking, trying to reflect his measured calm.

'Well you can't stay here.'

'Of course, I understand.'

She had been prepared for an argument.

'I mean, I know it's empty most of the year but it's not that simple. It's our family home.'

He nodded and looked slightly to her left out the window to the garden where the sound of the birds drifted in on a cool spring breeze.

'We will leave as soon as possible. Is Saturday ok? I will

need to make arrangements.'

Ciara was discommoded by his immediate acceptance of his fate. It softened her.

'I can give you until the end of the month.'

'That's very generous.'

She was put out. She was the one in the right here but this calm man made her feel like he was being the reasonable one, squatting in her home for months now.

'Right. Well, I suppose that's everything.'

'Thank you.'

'You're welcome.'

He walked her to the door. He was still acting like it was his house. She could feel her irritation rising again.

'Luke, get in the car.'

He trailed across, scuffing his shoes in the gravel.

'Mam, I don't want to go home. I want to stay here. I want to play with Lena.'

He squirmed and whined as she wrestled him into his car seat.

As she drove down the lane she looked in the rear view mirror. Lena stood at the door waving goodbye to Luke. Abdullah stood behind her, his hand resting gently on her brown curls. It was a gesture she remembered from her own father.

Oh fuck it. She began to reverse the car back up the lane. There was an arrangement to be made.

Bogeyman

By Ekaterina Crawford

Ekaterina was born and grew up in Moscow and now lives in Aldershot with her husband and their two children. She always loved writing but it's only in the past few years that she really pursued her passion. Ekaterina's creative pieces were published by the Visual Verse Anthology. She has won Writers' Forum Magazine Poetry Competition and was placed 3rd in short stories Competition. She has also won 2021 Kingston Libraries Short Stories Competition.

Bogeyman

Wrestled out of a hot and sweaty
dream, with my mouth still full
of its salty taste, I stare into
the dark corner of my room,

wide-eyed, as the shadows
begin their ritual dance. Lurking,
at the back of my room,
of my mind, they had lain in wait,

but now flooding in –
repressed memories of the past.
Your dark shadow in the dim
moving closer. Closer. Reaching,

where's sacred, you stale breath
fills the air and scalds my face.
On the bed, like on the altar, virgin's
sacrificed for blood, rough hands

touch where it's forbidden,
innocence nipped in the bud.
Thirty-odd years since, I remember
you only had to die to spur

the memories, of what had happened
of the evil monster that you were.
The coffin moves into the cremator,
and mother sobs squeezing my hand.

As you're engulfed and turn to ashes,
I pray to God, you burn in hell.

Her

By Alison Nuorto

An EFL Teacher living in Bournemouth but with a nomadic heart that yearns to roam far and wide. She feasts on horror stories and the traditional ghost stories of M. R. James and harbours an appreciation for the Macabre. Her poems have appeared in a handful of Anthologies and she was delighted to make the shortlist for the Bournemouth Writing Prize in 2021. Currently, she is working on producing an Anthology of her own, to promote awareness of male suicide. As long as she has a pulse, she hopes to always keep writing.

Her

'So…' Mark hesitated before looking down, 'who's this new man your mum's been seeing?'

'Oh, Rupert? He's great.' Jake replied, immediately toning down his enthusiasm upon spotting Mark's hurt expression.

'Rupert? That's a posh name, isn't it?' Mark exclaimed, not meaning to sound quite so jealous.

'Err, I guess so. Haven't really thought about it to be honest,' Jake replied, attempting to sound nonchalant. 'Well, we're both really excited about Bali.' Jake brightened. 'Mum's been buying loads of dresses. I bet she doesn't end up wearing half of them.'

'Bali? He's taking you to Bali?' Mark felt a sharp twinge in his chest.

'Yes, for two weeks. Oh Dad, I thought Mum had told you.'

The flash bastard, Mark thought to himself. The only place he'd ever managed to take them was to his Uncle Graham's mobile home in Dorset.

'It must be getting serious then,' Mark said softly, almost in a whisper.

'Well, he is round a lot, but Mum doesn't want him to move in just yet. She wants to make sure that we're both comfortable with it first.'

There was that sharp twinge again.

'So, why is he taking you both on holiday?' Inwardly, Mark prayed that this Rupert character wasn't intending to propose.

'He said it's a treat to celebrate my GCSE results.'

'I'm so proud of you, Son,' Mark instinctively ruffled Jake's hair, which clearly embarrassed him. 'I always knew you were bright. You definitely got your brains from your mum.'

'Thanks Dad,' Jake smiled.

Mark suddenly brightened. 'How about we plan a trip away? Just the two of us – father and son. Anywhere you like.'

'That sounds great, Dad. Yeah, let's do that.' Jake patted his father's shoulder reassuringly.

'Look, Jake ... I know I've said it before, but I'm sorry. I really am sorry.' Mark gazed into his son's eyes, as his eyes watered.

'It's okay, Dad, I understand.'

Mark acknowledged just how mature Jake was for his age. Far more sensible than he'd ever been, even as an adult. He really didn't deserve such a good son. He felt the sting of guilt every time he looked at this handsome, intelligent, and level-headed young man before him. His son was from a broken home because of his mistake. He'd given into temptation, and his momentary lapse of judgement had ruptured what had been a solid and happy marriage. His ex-wife only allowed him to see Jake on a whim when it suited her. He couldn't protest, because she'd been granted full custody. Now, some posh, loaded, cocky interloper had usurped his place at the table – and in his bed.

'Dad, you've lost weight and you're looking a bit gaunt. You're not ill, are you?' Jake looked concerned.

'No, I'm fine, Son. Just haven't been sleeping well. I think I'm just run down.'

'Are you eating properly? You've definitely lost weight.'

Mark laughed, 'who's the father here? It's okay, I'm fine, really. Don't worry.'

Jake smiled half-heartedly.

'Your mum... is she happy?' Mark asked tentatively after a brief silence.

Jake shifted in his seat. 'She was happy with you, Dad... but yes, she seems happy.'

Mark remembered when he and Jake's mum, Shelley, really had been happy. Childhood sweethearts, on their second day at Primary school, she'd splashed his face with blue paint. When she saw her handiwork, she painted her own nose blue so they would match.

This gesture made him vow to follow this angelic, slightly clumsy, red-haired beauty anywhere. They'd struggled financially after Jake was born, but they'd always been on the same page, and were determined to give him the best education they could provide. Their situation began to improve when he'd secured a pay rise, and Shelley was embarking on setting up her own mobile Beauty business. They hadn't been able to afford a holiday abroad, but his dream of a fly drive holiday to the States was tantalisingly close to being realised. During a quiet lull in the office, he would close his eyes and imagine their beaming faces as they tore along Route 66 in the American sunshine.

That was before his moment of weakness drove a giant wedge between them. They had stayed together – for Jake – but Shelley had struggled to contain her resentment and anger. How could he blame her? Their robotic love making destroyed them both.

'I can't get her out of my head. When we're intimate, I wonder if you're thinking about her, if it's her you see when you're kissing me... touching me. She's always going to be a spectre, haunting this marriage.'

There was nothing that Mark could say to that. Silence seemed preferable to feeble protestations.

'I still love you,' she'd said one evening, after one of their habitual arguments, 'but the respect has gone,' she'd added, sadly.

Mark looked at Jake affectionately. He felt heartened by his son's concern for his wellbeing. He was reluctant to reveal the reason behind his poor sleep quality. The nightmares had started up again. The guilt fuelled dreams that had started just before he and Shelley had decided to part ways. He'd wake up shaking and drenched in sweat. It was a detail that he'd intentionally kept from his son. He'd always slept poorly, so Jake hadn't pressed him further. The nightmares were so vivid and realistic, they were almost an accurate account of his act of foolishness.

It was an unusually warm afternoon in April. He had the day off and was on his way to collect Jake from school. He'd decided to stop and get some roses for Shelley, as a surprise. Waiting in line at the florists, he couldn't help but notice the young girl in front of him. He guessed that she was about twenty-one. Her waist length, blonde hair shimmered in the sunlight that streamed in, and he got a hint of apple and Jasmine. She was wearing a maxi yellow sundress that made her behind look temptingly pinchable, he'd decided. He felt himself getting hard and held the roses strategically so nobody would notice. He was so transfixed by her figure, he didn't notice when her transaction finished, and she turned around to catch him mid ogle. He was mortified but she'd smiled, tilted her head to one side and run her long fingers through her tresses.

Back in the car, Mark was on cloud nine. He'd certainly enjoyed his encounter with the sexy nymph at the florists, but he was also waiting on an important call from the office. Probably one of the most important calls of his life. He was up for promotion, and his supervisor had promised to call him with the outcome before the end of the day. Based on the glowing feedback from his most recent appraisal, it seemed to be in the bag, but still, Mark knew from experience never to count his chickens. He'd been on tenterhooks all day. Nothing but nervous energy – and more recently, arousal. He checked his phone: no calls or messages.

When he stopped at the traffic lights, he spotted her. The temptress from the florists was waiting to cross. His eyes were roaming over her curves as his phone began vibrating furiously. They darted to the screen, and he saw that it was work. He should have ignored it but felt that it would make him look bad.

He answered just to let them know that he was driving and that he'd be home in ten minutes. His supervisor agreed, and he promptly ended the call. In his nerves fuelled haste, he neglected to check that the lights had changed. He was still looking down at his phone when he put his foot on the pedal. There was the most unnatural sound, and he assumed that a tyre had blown out, until he recognised the Pre-Raphealite tresses splayed across his windscreen and the flimsy summer dress that billowed across his bonnet like a sail.

'I have to go now, Dad. You will take care of yourself, won't you?'

Mark smiled grimly, nodding weakly.

'I'll visit again, soon, I promise,' Jake added. 'I'll try to persuade Mum to come next time,' he called out hopefully as an afterthought, as a guard ushered him out.

'Time, what a strange concept,' Mark pondered to himself. Some people would give their eyeteeth to have more, while others have far too much. As for him, now, he had nothing but time.

Vespers

By Craig B McClure

Craig was born in Edinburgh but his career as a chef has taken him south where he now lives. He has been writing poetry for only the last two years after leaving his profession for personal reasons. Having involved himself with a writing group this is his first entry to competition.

Vespers

Deus in adjutorium meum intende
O God come to my assistance
For though we travel together
We are strangers of infinite faiths
Branches of the same tree
Cast into this journey by desire
We pray, we cry, we hope
Here on this frothing sea fury
On flimsy flotsam inflatables
Bone freezing, skin tingling
As salty spray spits in our faces
Huddled, hunched in desperation
In search of a world without torment
For we are but children of chance
Orphaned from our homelands
Escaping our purgatory
In acid anticipation of a future

Fending off the furies
Tossed on this torrid tempest
Starlight coruscated on wave tips
Guiding us on, escaping the fear
Eyes blurred by saline tears
As we gain the naked shoreline
My God has smiled on me
Helper of the helpless
Unloose the bonds of guilt within
Resolve culpae vinculum
Amen, alleluia

The Prescription

By Terry Kerins

Terry Kerins was born in Macroom in Co. Cork, Ireland and studied Pharmacy in Trinity College, Dublin. Terry enjoys reading fiction and has been writing short stories for many years. After taking a break for a few sleep-deprived years, after becoming a mother, she has rekindled her love and interest in writing and is reworking older pieces and writing new short stories and flash fiction. She lives in Cork city with her daughter.

The Prescription

It was as if a bag of wet sand had lodged on her chest and, with each breath, got heavier and heavier, until it felt like her ribcage was no longer strong enough to keep lifting it up and down.

Dr. Griffin wrote her a prescription: antibiotics, steroids, an inhaler and the Xanax.

'The steroids can disrupt your sleep, let me give you something to help while you're on them. Xanax is a relaxant, it'll calm you down a bit as well until your breathing improves,' he'd said.

Sleep had been a problem long before the chest infection. It seemed that her life had become one big angry cry of 'Mammy!' Sometimes, after a whole train of 'Mammies,' she'd snap 'round, 'What?' only to hear one of the children say, 'nothing,' and burst out laughing or crying, depending on the flavour of the day. That was, in contrast to Stephen. He said less and less. The spaces between his words stretched out and they were soon long enough to fit whole sentences. These created voids big enough for whole conversations to fall into. His body was still there, his mass an obstacle to get around in the house, but the longer the silences went on, the more he folded in on himself, his words and thoughts wound tight around him like a straitjacket.

Her chest got better, the antibiotics and steroids worked their magic, as did the Xanax. Shortly after taking one, it felt as if she was closing the door in a quiet dark room, shutting herself in to be able to shut down, to lose herself in sleep. It was such a respite. Once the steroid dose was finished, there was still a card and a half of the relaxants left. She put them in the zipper pocket of her handbag, ready to drop back to the pharmacy.

But the nights kept her awake. Stephen panned out in the bed beside her, tired after his day on the farm, an immovable boulder taking up more than his fair share of the space. The kids no longer needed her at night for feeds or cuddles. Sleep: it was what she'd longed for when they were smaller, but now it would not come. It would lower, start to settle, but then her heart would pinch, her whole body would jerk, leaving her wide awake again. The pale, blue wisp of hovering sleep frightened away by her desperation and neediness.

The curtains in their bedroom were thin. They'd replaced his parents blue and brown floral ones after the wedding. She'd chosen a maroon colour, remembering how exciting the decorating project had been. She hated the curtains now, any bit of light in the mornings turned the room into a raw pink cavity, like waking up inside of a mouth.

'Blackouts? What would we want those for?' he'd said when she'd suggested a change, 'sure we're in the middle of the fields, there's no one to be looking in on us.'

One night, a few weeks later, as Stephen lay on his back taking deep snorting breaths, she remembered the Xanax. Her bag was on the hook at the back of the bedroom door, and she took it to the bathroom. The bulb hummed and slime forming around the bar of soap by the sink caught her eye, a green upset against the white enamel. The zip-lock sleeve was still in the inside pocket of her handbag; thirteen tablets left. Biting one in half, she tucked the remaining half back into its foil cocoon. She washed it down with water from the toothbrush mug and went back to their room. For the first time in weeks, calmness spread, her body sunk below the level of the mattress, her brain formed a full stop and gorgeous sleep took over.

The next day, Jane was extra careful driving the

kids to school, remembering the warning label: 'May cause drowsiness, take care when driving or operating machinery'. The last time she'd taken them, it had been at home to recover from the 'nearly pneumonia' as Dr. Griffin had called it. But up and about that day, the call of 'Mammy!' didn't seem as grating, nor did the broad wall of her husband's back as he washed his hands in the kitchen sink before dinner. She could block out the squelching his hands made as he lathered them, his muck merging with the mud from the potatoes in the colander, leading a greasy brown stream down the plughole.

That night, she took the other half, *best not to return half tablets to the pharmacy*. She'd swing by the next day and drop off the rest, a nice even dozen, or maybe even just wash them down the sink herself to save the trip.

But somehow, neither happened and, almost as if by their own accord, the tablets dwindled, until one night there was only one half left. She popped it in her mouth, chewing it straight – it worked faster that way, its gritty bitter taste soon to be replaced by sweet indifference.

After dropping the children to school the next day, she made her way to the GP's surgery in the village.

'Hello, I'm wondering if I can make an appointment to see Dr. Griffin?'

'Oh, I'm afraid he's off this week. We have a locum, Dr. Rasheed, do you want to see him?'

Jane fiddled with the belt on her coat, 'yes, okay.'

'Just take a seat in his office, he'll be with you in a minute.'

Jane looked around the small room, remembering the last time she'd been there, struggling for breath. She remembered focusing on the poster of a pregnant woman, cupping her bump, smiling in an ignorant-to-what-was-to-come way that only came with a first pregnancy. The poster was gone, replaced by a step-by-step guide to correct handwashing technique.

Dr. Rasheed was young and wore pointy shoes, 'hello, Jane? I'm Dr. Rasheed,' he said with a perfectly formed Cork accent. 'How can I help you today?'

Jane held her breath for a moment before answering, 'it's for a repeat prescription.'

'Right,' the doctor frowned at the screen. 'Hmm... I don't see any regular medication.'

Her mind went back to a previous visit and the rash in the creases of her elbows that had brought her there, Dr. Griffin saying to just re-order the cream if needed.

'It's for the cream, and...' she added, 'the inhaler, you know, the blue one.'

'Right...'

'And, oh yes, the tablets that help with the breathing,' she said, gripping on to her hands to keep them steady. 'You see, I'd a bad chest, Dr. Griffin said they'd help when I'm feeling caught up.'

She took a raggedy breath as if to prove her point. Jane felt a blush filling up her cheeks and her eyes went to the poster again. *How, if Stephen spent so much time soaping and scrubbing, did his nails never seem fully clean, always with a furrow of earth under each one?*

The young doctor was focused on the PC.

'Okay, well, I don't see that on your file, but sometimes Dr. Griffin does handwritten notes,' he said, tapping the computer monitor as if it was somehow to blame. 'I'll give you a prescription for twelve tablets, but if you still feel short of breath or a bit panicky, please make a follow up appointment.'

'Thanks Doctor.'

A few weeks later, there was only one tablet left again.

She took them whole now. Back in the consultation room, one corner of the handwashing poster was starting to curl up against the light green wall.

Dr. Griffin was back and quizzed her, 'would you say you are feeling joy in everyday life? Have you lost interest in your friends, your social life?'

What friends? What social life?

She pictured their sitting room when the kids were in bed: Stephen ploughing through a packet of chocolate digestives in front of the nine o'clock news, spraying crumbs as he shot curses at the meteorologist when he said the wrong thing.

'No, nothing like that, it's just the breath, I find the Xanax help with it.'

He made her blow through a cardboard tube, once, twice, three times, took her blood pressure and looked into the back of her eyes with a small torch.

He tapped away on the keyboard.

'Breathlessness is distressing, Jane, try to get out, do a bit of exercise, maybe register for yoga in the community hall,' he said, before handing over the prescription at last. 'Some people find they get dependent on these; just watch how you go with them.'

She watched all right, as the little purple tablets counted down faster this time. 'A dental appointment' was her muffled line to Stephen the next time as she held on to her jaw. He frowned and handed over a fifty euro note, flicking it with his thumb and finger to make sure it was just one. Jane took it, hand unsteady, and went straight to the Corolla in the yard. The car indicated left for the village, but she continued past the shabby Colgate-smelling room that housed Dentist Carey and drove to the city.

The 24/7 walk-in GP clinic was on the quay. It was mostly made of glass and the watery sunlight reflected off it, bouncing spits of light off its corners, blinding Jane as she tried to read the bell number. The girl at reception had hostile, red nails filed to a point, and they clanked on the surface of the desk every time she moved her hands. She gave Jane a clipboard with a 'new patient' form to fill out and offered her a bottle of sparkling water. Jane fumbled with the clipboard, the pen, and the frigid water bottle. It rolled along the submarine grey carpet and came to a stop at a chrome table-leg. Jane sat and, once the form was filled in and the bottle safely parked on the table, she looked around the room. A single frame of what must be art, if money was no object, hung on the waiting room wall, and there was no mention of handwashing. Everything looked so clean, correct handwashing technique was a given here.

Eighty euro later, Jane was back in the car in the multi-storey carpark. The prescription was typed out, but at the bottom there was a hand-written, 'repeat by one', followed by a squiggle and a sequence of numbers all joined together and slanting down the page. She found a black biro in the glove box and changed the 'one' into a 'nine' before folding the paper and tucking it in the zipper pocket of her purse. There was a late-night pharmacy beside ALDI, they'd fill it there for her on the way home.

Over Christmas, Stephen's brother and sisters and their families were all squeezed around the table, talking about the crops and the yield and the size of the turkey. The kitchen was too hot and too small for so many people and it took one and a half tablets to get her to the same level of calm. She'd started off with just one, but somewhere between mass, with the reluctant children fidgeting beside her in the pew, and the endless requests for cups of tea or 'something stronger' afterwards, she'd bitten another half tablet off while in the downstairs loo. Carrying them around in her apron pocket was safest, especially with the younger kids in the house for the day.

The meal was late, it was nearly half past three before they sat down. She could feel her guests getting anxious, hovering and picking at the bowl of potato stuffing, her mother-in-law's recipe, 'especially for Stephen'. She'd been told it was his favourite that first year and now it was expected, even though Jane herself had always preferred a bread stuffing, loaded with onions, butter and herbs. Her in-laws all thought they had a right to sit and be waited upon, just because they'd sat at the same table every day as children and eaten breakfast there. Stephen sat in his father's seat and, when he did the honours and carved the bird, his brother and sisters clapped. The children joined in, Jane's hands were full with the bowl of roast potatoes.

Once the plates were loaded, she drank the festive glass of red quickly. The mound of brown and beige food on the plate in front of her looked unappealing. A gravy coated brussel sprout lay abandoned on the tablecloth. *Later on, it'll be murder to get the stain out.* The wine on top of the Xanax made her able to sit through the meal, slightly removed from the racket and the clatter. She felt held in a heavy velvet hammock. The talk and emotions bounced off her and doubled back to strike those around her at the table in an invisible tennis rally.

After dinner, while alone doing the washing-up, she poured more of the wine into a reindeer mug belonging to one of the kids and drank it in one go. Rinsing the mug, she watched the reindeers circling around it, galloping, galloping, galloping on a pointless treadmill. The mug would soon be put away until next year, only to be taken out again so they could continue on their dead-end merry-go-round. She wondered if the mug would retain the taste of the wine and whether the next hot chocolate would sense its unfaithfulness.

'Silly notions,' she said under her breath and turned off the kitchen light behind her.

The rest of the adults were glued to *Mrs. Brown's Boys* in the sitting-room. The children were in the den, worn out from the early start and the added chaos the cousins brought. She looked at Stephen and saw him as he was before. Before his father's death and his mother's insistence that he 'defer for a year'. Before the boundary issue and the trouble with the neighbours, before the two blue lines and the hurried wedding, before the coldness crept in. She saw him at the Debs, tanned from a season of football, in his rented tuxedo, ready to go to Dublin. Now his check shirt strained to close, his middle spilling over the belt of his trousers, and there was a hole in the toe of one of his socks. He caught her looking at it and slid his foot over the carpet, so the flabby sock rolled the hole under his foot.

'Anyone for a top-up?' He asked, looking straight at her and for one minute, it seemed like Stephen could see through it all as well. But dullness settled behind his eyes, his mouth sealed closed. He went around the room with the bottle, filling his brother and sisters' glasses, their spouses', his own and, by the time he came to her, there was none left. He stood in front of her with the empty bottle in his hand. He held it out and put it in hers before turning and sitting back down in the chair nearest the fire.

Jane's eyes smarted, his own glass was full well past the little white line on it that measured 'a unit'. He'd come back from the Co-op one day with a box of six. She'd been delighted, her mind jumping to something luxurious, a rare present, only to discover a set of half a dozen 'Drink Safely' wine glasses: 'On sale, going for half nothing'. They used them when visitors came over, which wasn't often, and she turned the white line to the opposite side, hoping no one would notice it.

Jane got up, went to the cold back kitchen, and put the empty bottle in the recycling. She stood at the narrow, single paned window by the back door and looked into the Christmas night; into the stillness. At the end of the yard stood the hayshed, a hulk of a structure, the light on its gable end cast a dirty orange glow in the muddy paddock. *Far from a Christmas welcome,* she thought as she strained her eyes to see past it, to look deeper into the night. But beyond was just blackness.

She took a step back from the window and it filled up with the reflection of her own face, distorted like a stroke victim against the muzz of drizzle at the other side of the glass. Her hand found the sheet of Xanax and her fingers released one into her palm. She saw it in the jarring light of the bare bulb, saw her choices, saw her no choices. She could put it back, grind the remainder of the tablets in the garlic press and be done with them. Honour her vows, show up at community centre for yoga. But instead, she put it on her tongue and chewed until it was just an unpleasant aftertaste swallowed in a dry gulp.

She turned and faced the sitting-room, the door was ajar as the fire was too hot for the mild evening. Stephen had built it up too far and it licked the sides of the hearth with its greedy tongues, swallowing all the freshness in the room. Her husband's head turned, seeing her in the hall, waiting for her to go back to take her place. It would soon be time for tea and turkey sandwiches, she'd have to cut the Christmas cake and the tin of sweets would be passed around again.

Echo Land

By Celeste Engel

Celeste Engel completed a Masters in Writing for the Media at Bournemouth University in 2011. Celeste has had three short films produced. She has directed six multi-media plays; was shortlisted for the Kenneth Branagh Writing Prize in 2015 for her play SHINE BRIGHT her play SWEET DREAMS received a development package from Theatre West in 2021. Since 2012 Celeste has been working at the Arts University Bournemouth on the Filmmaking Short Course.

Echo Land

Like the prodigal
I returned
Arrived back to place and people
Vibrant in my colouring
To discover I had become,
A ghost
A whisper
A haunting as I haunted
An echo of moments past
A dream one struggles to remember
I no longer knew where I was
Navigated my way like a bat
Using past echoes to feel my way through worlds
I travelled time
My lungs led me to Air
Tumbled me away like a weed
I found myself dancing on new winds
A tornado tidal with expectation
The voices, the faces, the violence of your places
You storied me to sleep
The missing, an ache
A whole perforated by absence
I empty lying foetal in new world humming
I gaze back, tie myself to you tight
Lie in sleep, yet walk days unnumbered
Scream through one way mirror, invisible
I the dream, the echo
A whisper, indecipherable
The dappled light of sparkled diamond memory
Whose tales have you returning to memorised phrase

Morning light brings a clarity that exiles the fog
I sang your waves in and called your waves out
Paused your tidal pull on a whim
Made your waves crash with an arm swish boom
That was when, I was home...home was you
Home was then, I will never be at home again
I am a prism made up of mirrored shards
Reflecting light whilst straining against the glass
I am the dew evaporated by morning sun
Loss tints my gaze and colours all I see
A cacophony of hues make up my symphony
I am a ghost in a country full of spectres

Immigrants

By Laila Lock

Laila Lock is currently studying for a Master's Degree in Creative Writing at Bournemouth University. She lives with my family and an eclectic range of animals in Dorset.

Immigrants

He called me Sister and my heart pixelated.
A week later a vine field message.
"This is the land of your fathers
And my daughters in a row."

I had been unmoored for a while
Needed to align

With four daughters in a row.
Stood in azure shallows.
Up to their knees in blousa and jeans
Chaining me in to where
The white shells sparkle
In their curly hair
And the corals had always waved
Since he left
That city by the sea.

My Brother loves the rain,
Justice, and the countryside.
I am his own mirror,
once removed
In the agricultural college.

They said, "Why are you here?"
Odd choice for a girl.
But Dad didn't tell me
About the track that led to
Cooled, tiled courtyards and soft soled
Grandad waiting for him on that lonely
Farm forever.

Only the time he sold the gummer sheep
As gimmers in the market behind
Old Grandad's back.
Who, shame red, hit him with a stick.

Dad needed Paris and dances
And the university on a hill
Behind the farm.
But I, by carrying innocent buckets
and planting the seed
Went home for him.

The Rediscovery of Fire

By Chris Wright

Chris Wright is a writer from Bangor, Northern Ireland. He has been longlisted for the Irish Book Awards Short Story of the Year, was runner-up in The Mairtín Crawford Award, and his work has featured in several print anthologies and publications. Chris is currently studying for an MA in Creative Writing at Queen's University, Belfast.

The Rediscovery of Fire

The Rediscovery of Fire

John Dalton was a statue at the side of the stage; his head bowed; eyes closed tight in a silent prayer to a God he didn't believe in. He wasn't praying for help in his performance or for the music to inhabit him the way it always had before. No, John prayed for the right type of audience. One that would appreciate the nuance of his movements, the subtlety of the fluctuations of his throat, the story told in the contraction of muscles around his ageing eyes. He prayed for the crowd to become a part of him, something he could flex and stretch and mould to his will.

The band lingered behind him. Far behind him. Tony Lucas, the drummer with the blonde locks as lustrous as at their first gig – that long gone basement bar in Liverpool that stank of stale beer and piss, back when they were called Warship Cancer and Billy was still alive and slapping the Bass like a fucking God – leaned against the wall, twirling a stick in his right hand, laughing with his head thrown back, mouth wide and baring teeth as white as sin. Danny Magill – wearing his now legendary bowler hat and braces like a cowboy barman – shook with laughter as he recounted to Tony an overcompensating tale of sex and debauchery from the glory days that weren't glory days to the rest of the band as Billy had died and Danny, his replacement, was barely out of school during the actual glory days. Tony knew the story well. He was there. Yet, every time he heard it, he treated it as if it were the first time. That was Tony's gift.

Danny's eyes flicked towards a roadie carrying his bass on stage to set it stage left, beside his mic; the one that was never turned on. John insisted on it. Their voices didn't harmonise well, and he thought the result was too muddy.

'Two minutes,' the stagehand said, holding up two

95

fingers in case the words were not enough to penetrate the relentless whistle of John's tinnitus.

John started his pre-gig routine. Mantras, breathing, stretching; it was like the mating dance of an African bird. Tony flicked his head towards John, one eyebrow raised mockingly. Danny snickered. It was gig 200 of their final world tour – their fifth final tour to be exact, but who's counting – and they had watched this display 200 times in a row. It was an amalgam of every pre-gig routine John had been performing for the last 30 years. It hurt his old bones to do it, but still, he insisted even though it was of no actual benefit to him.

'Fuck's sake, John the Baptist doin' his wee-wee dance again?' Peter Barnes said in his Brummie drawl as he sauntered over, shoulders loose, arms swinging. He had the heavy-eyed face of a sad, cartoon dog and a voice to match. He wore his black waistcoat, no shirt, his body still wiry with twisted muscle like it was when he was seventeen.

John finished his final mantra and turned to face his band. His eyes were drawn to Peter's abs, then down to his own gut, hidden behind a flowy shirt, open from the chest up. His balding head hid beneath a pork-pie hat, and long, thin strands of hair hung down from the rim like wet noodles. It was fooling no-one. They'd all seen the pap shots where he looked like Donald Trump in a wind tunnel.

'Ladies and Gentlemen, give it up for the Haunted Maniacs!' the announcer screamed, taking them by surprise.

John still cringed every time he heard their name. He never liked it but reluctantly agreed when he was challenged to come up with something better and had nothing. Then they made it big, and it stuck. To him, it always sounded contrived, despite the words long since losing their individual meaning and becoming synonymous with the band, like The Rolling Stones or The Beatles. Then again, things always look different from within than without. It's like the more bizarre parts of Quantum Theory, which, incidentally, was the band name John had thought of long after the conversation was over.

The war-shell explosion of the crowd pulled John from his internal grumbles. He stepped out onto stage with no regard for his band mates. He waved, he blew kisses, he resented every bastard crammed into the auditorium.

He knew what was coming. An F chord. That one fucking chord. So simple written down. On its own, it was nothing. Play it on a 1967 Bower Lancashire Deluxe Organ and it had power. It influenced people. It had residency in the minds of a huge swathe of the population. It elicited a Pavlovian response in those of a certain age who had heard it again and again and, without really understanding why, immediately knew what it signified. The start of their biggest hit, 'Wasted Teen'.

John always opened with it. Most thought it was to set the scene, get the gig going with a bang. Really, he just wanted it out of the way, given the deeply conflicted feelings he had about the song. It stirred something inside him much as it did the fans.

He sat himself down in front of his faithful organ and rubbed his hand along it like he was stroking the silky fray of a lover's hair. They would make beautiful music together no matter if the band were speaking to him that week. He stretched gnarled fingers towards the keys. He knew exactly how they would feel against his skin before making contact with them, which made the familiarity, the electricity of touch, exhilarating.

He gave a cursory glance around to ensure everyone was in position. He spread his fingers and placed them in preparation for the music about to flow through him. He took a deep breath, for he knew what magic would appear when he released that fucking chord, both within and without.

He hit that infamous F chord and unleashed a tidal wave.

A wash of adrenaline rinsed through the crowd as soon as their ears could take in the sound waves to identify and interpret them. The recognition was fibre quick. It moved like electricity through wire, dopamine through blood, forcing out a roar of excitement as if the crowd were a single entity, an animal waking from slumber. The excitement bounced back to the band. They felt it too, the sheer elation their music could incite, even more powerful filtered through the sound of one fucking chord.

But there was also a downside to that one fucking chord.

While it wasn't their first hit, it was the one that rocketed them to the top, put their smooth, putty faces on every pop magazine, every music show, every TV there was way back in 1974. It had started it all, and John had once loved it, back when he was still living with his mum in a two up two down terraced house in East London – his dad was an infamous bank robber and bare-knuckle boxer who was serving an 8-10 stretch for assault and battery in Wandsworth Prison when the song came out.

John, like most young men, had a fractious relationship with his father. He was never the tough-skinned youth that his dad had wanted. He was quiet, studious, thoughtful, and slow to a fight – mainly because he couldn't beat Casey's Drum as his auld Irish Ma used to say in a kindly, matter of fact way with no notion that it flayed him raw. While his dad wanted him down at the local boxing club, taking on the street rats that he spent more time with than his own son, John would rather spend time with his ma, down at the local Baptist church. She was their resident organ player and, while they couldn't afford one at home, they gave her free reign to practise anytime she liked. Saturday morning, she would sit young John on her knee, place his little chubby digits on the keys and push them down with her own, pointed fingers until the music leeched into his soul. She wasn't an overly affectionate woman, so this was heaven to the young boy. So much so, he even repurposed the opening of her favourite hymn, 'It Came Upon a Midnight Clear,' for his greatest achievement, yet no one noticed. Not even his mum.

As he slipped more and more under the spell of music, he never saw the strange contradiction in his drift from evangelical music to rock and roll. For John, music was his rebellion against the violent wants and expectations of his father. Yet, the further he fell into it, and into rebellion itself, the more he entered the realms of his wayward father; dive bars, scabby fights, flinging beer and spitting far.

This song that launched them into the stratosphere, 'Wasted Teen', started out life as a twenty-seven-minute opening to a Sci-Fi Rock Opera John had written called 'Tam Buckland and his Adventures in the Wastelands of Deep Space', which took deep inspiration from the old pulp serials he watched as a kid, such as Universal's 'Buck Rogers'. He began playing segments from his self-proclaimed masterpiece to the local teens in the hope of word spreading about his glorious rise to fame. They laughed.

Among the rosy faces that burst out laughing, one remained straight. It belonged to a young man with long blonde hair and a flair for rhythm who had the idea of taking the work John had already done and breaking it down into song-length segments for an experimental album. John scoffed at first but, after a few meetings in the Baptist – John 'liberating' the keys from his ma's knicker drawer – they found a synergy, a connection that neither of them had ever felt. They connected on a sonic wavelength, like the atoms that made them vibrated at the same frequency.

A direct distillation of these days flowed through John upon the implementation of that chord. It was a feeling he often forgot outside of the moment, taking him by surprise every time. Yet, it was the very thing that kept him coming back as, like most adults, he was always trying to recreate the heady, oscillating joy of youth; when your senses were dialled to eleven and everything was the end of a world or the beginning of a universe, and the whole thing pickled in the fermented fruit of intense sexual awakening.

John flashed a look towards Tony who sat ready with his drumsticks aloft, the tight sinew in his arms pulsating with his heartbeat, beads of sweat forming on his head like fish scales. He saw the very thing he couldn't see a minute ago, his best friend.

He smiled. Tony smiled back. They were both on that first stage in Liverpool. They had everything in front of them, the good, the bad, and the ugly.

The first tour, the drink, the drugs, the girls, the boys, the big fight that nearly ended them, the new direction, Billy's death, the experimental solo years, the reunion, Danny's introduction, the restart, the return to old, the rediscovery of fire, the old feelings, the love, the hate, the distillation of their entire lives blasted through speakers, conveyed by one fucking chord. One chord that soon turned into another and another, followed by the first flair of drums; sweat flicking from long locks, energy surging through ageing muscle.

More flooded into John as the music flowed out. Creating together, destroying together, an arm around a shoulder at the right time, a flaming row fuelled by the conflict that can only be borne of love and mutual respect. Newborns held proudly, truths told meekly, standing shoulder to shoulder at bedsides and gravesides, bringing pleasure and pain to the world and each other.

John turned to the crowd; to his mum, his dad, the street rats he didn't want to fight, the ones he did. The teens watching him play in his garage, dressed from head to toe in silver, as they laugh, him burning inside, forgetting the bursting feeling of pure creativity when writing – when even the drugs he hadn't touched in nearly two decades seemed as part of the process as they made him feel good, and they made him feel bad, the same as everything else in the glittering world of rock and roll.

John put his lips to the mic, the rough kiss of it a coldness he would never want to forget.

'I'd like to introduce you to a man you already know,' John announced as the rest of the band idled the song: 'my best friend, my brother, my other, my partner in music, Mister Tony Lucas.'

A roar that would make the world shiver swept the auditorium. Tony started slow – tap tap tiss, tap tap tiss – before breaking into a thundering drum solo worthy of the Greek gods themselves. John laughed, his hand still aloft, fingers flat and pointing straight towards Tony. He moved his hand in a sweeping motion towards Danny.

'Next up, on bass, Mister Danny Magill.'

Danny plucked a mini-solo before shouting 'thank you' to the crowd, and when the sound didn't echo out in front of him, he remembered the mic wasn't switched on. He muttered a few choice words, just for John.

'On lead guitar, Mister Peter Barnes.'

Peter's leathery fingers flicked from string to string with an effortless zeal. John watched it as he always did, with a tight blip of jealousy in his gut. Peter's fingers worked in another dimension from the rest of him, like God was reaching through a portal and working the strings himself. The crowd roared as he threw himself about.

Tony rolled his eyes. Danny smiled an exasperated smile and John just shook his head. There was little malice in their reactions, rather an acknowledgement of a man just being himself. They were seventeen again, watching him do it for the first time in a near empty pub. No matter where they were, Peter always played like it was Wembley Arena on the last night of the tour, which it now happened to be.

Tony and Danny joined in, raising the sound to a wonderful crescendo. Tony leaned into his mic to finish off the introduction.

'And finally, a man who needs no introduction... so I'm not going to give him one...' he smiled at John. 'The one, the only, Mister John Dalton.'

John's fingers hurt as he rattled the keys, trying to recreate sounds first made in his bedroom as a kid, refined over decades of shows and recordings. He stumbled a few times, but the crowd didn't notice, as he had taken those stumbles and reconstituted them into intentional flourish before slipping, full circle, back to the start of their biggest hit. Back to that one fucking chord that lifted the crowd to another level. He could feel the heat coming off them, he could smell them in the air, the noise they made; primal, primordial, like the first man to stretch skin over wood and slap it with a hairy hand, laughing and looking to his peers for approval of his invention. Back when things could be invented rather than just rediscovered.

On Kerrera Island

By Sharon Black

Sharon Black is from Glasgow and lives in a remote valley of the Cévennes mountains. Her poetry is published widely and has won many prizes. Her collections are To Know Bedrock (Pindrop, 2011), The Art of Egg (Two Ravens, 2015; Pindrop, 2019), and a pamphlet, Rib (Wayleave, 2021). Her third and fourth full collections will appear in 2022 with Vagabond Voices and Drunk Muse Press respectively, www.sharonblack.co.uk

On Kerrera Island

This morning, I'm hiking
in the hills of Andalusia, figs dripping
from the trees,

pomegranates splitting on hot limestone rocks
amid the scrub, miles from any road.
I'm striding, dusty,

beside a *Nationale*
somewhere in the *Midi*, my hitching thumb
hooked firmly round my rucksack strap,

I've dropped behind my friends
on Rannoch Moor, damp from sweat
and midge spray, ten miles in,

another six to reach our lodge
along the Way
that keeps dipping, re-emerging.

I'm everywhere I've ever
walked alone, exhausted, aching
with some twinge or injury

and nothing but to keep on walking,
until the rawness sings
more softly, each moment passing

to the next as the spirit disengages
from its capable machine,
pulse playing out

against a drop that could be anywhere,
each step any step, no difference
between a footfall and a life.

Elizabeth's Melody

By Carrie Griffiths

A mature student at Bournemouth Uni, Carrie is in her final year of a BA in English. She would like to continue writing short stories and eventually publish the contemporary gothic horror novel she is currently writing for her dissertation. She also hopes to gain a Masters in Creative Writing and Publishing. Carrie devotes her free time to writing, editing, and supporting other writers through her blogs in fandom-based communities.

Elizabeth's Melody

A shallow sigh left his lips. He revelled in the pleasurable feeling of muscle against the nape of her neck. Wisps of flaxen hair bustled in all directions, as uncontrollable as the changeable autumn day. The skin of her neck tugged against her clavicle as she rolled her slender neck upwards, resting on his shoulder, and watching sycamore seeds dally through the air. He placed his hand on the protrusion in her lower belly, nuzzling her ear, the scent of petrichor and warm pomegranate littering her skin.

'Don't think I've forgotten.' He bit gently on her earlobe and chuckled.

She sat and peered at him curiously, letting out a burst of high-pitched laughter, her eyes golden and dancing, shimmering like heat on a sun-baked road.

'You shouldn't be here. Not yet,' she said.

Opening her mouth, she bared gums greyed with putrefying rot, vomiting a clouded vision of absurd memories. Not those of happiness, but of regretful times, times where he'd hurt her, times when he'd made her feel like nothing.

The desire to flee walloped him in the gut. The ground rocked and splintered beneath him, falling away, creating a fissure in the earth.

They both fell together.

He gained purchase, dangling by one hand, his fingers embedded in brittle lacewood grain. His other hand released hers without thought, and she fell through greyed cotton, emerald foliage, into a stinging and slimed leaf nightfall.

He found himself suspended, hanging there over the chasm, his hand chafed by barbs, legs encased in brambles.

His wits, those he still recognised, were balanced on the gyroplane of a seedling that rotated past his face as if taunting him.

His grasp loosened, and he began to slip.

The bookcase jarred, aggravated.

'Dad, what are you doing at the window?' Elizabeth asked as she cleaned the crumbs from a leather wingback chair, hopping over the elderly tortoiseshell cat. Robert the Bruce, who moved faster than expected, almost tripped her.

'The cigarette factory is working hard again.' He stopped humming a tune and peered out from behind the net curtains. 'I smell it all the time,' he said, absently.

Elizabeth frowned. If a cigarette factory were producing its product, it would hardly be sending the smoke out through its chimneys. She slapped a throw pillow and shook her head with a sigh. The odour was probably from the neighbour with the discoloured jardinière drapes.

'Come and sit down, Dad. I'll cook you some dinner.'

She closed the window, took him by the elbow and led him to the easy chair. He struggled with those few steps, his feet shuffling, indenting the pile with his green embroidered slippers. They were a gift from the care home manager; he wasn't allowed shoes since he'd absconded over the fence and become lost in the village. She later found him waiting for a bus at a decaying stop that had last serviced the area in 1982.

'I'm not hungry, Charlotte,' he replied, turning on the TV to the local news.

She heard the low rumbling chatter of a conversation between the hosts but filtered out the white noise.

Opening the kitchen cupboards she'd restocked only yesterday, Elizabeth gulped back tears that hit her with such ferocity they almost overwhelmed her. Charlotte had been her father's sister. Not being recognised by one's parent is like a stab to the heart from one of the Jacobean swords she'd carefully removed from his belongings when he'd moved into Mount House.

A crumpled bag from a large granary loaf lay on the worktop. The crumbs on his chair now made sense. He'd eaten it all.

She cleared her throat.

'Daddy, what happened to the bread?'

'There is no bread, Charlotte. Anya will get some on her way home from work.'

Elizabeth leaned her head against the cupboard, using the MDF to cool her flushed face. She clenched her fists. Anya had been his father's first wife, a Spanish woman he'd met as a young man travelling in Barcelona before gaining his doctorate in psychology. Her throat felt blocked as she realised that he didn't remember her mother, who'd died only a few weeks before following forty years of marriage.

The situation with the bread reminded her of the sausage incident. It had occurred on the day of their mother's funeral, after Elizabeth had driven him back to Mount House. Her father had placed two packets of sausages under the gas grill and forgotten them, causing much smoke and a complete evacuation, though, luckily, not setting fire to the kitchen. At 8pm, when Elizabeth was about to take a sedative and go to bed, she received a call from the home advising her that the fire brigade had been called. Driving five miles, she had arrived to find her father refusing to leave his supported flat, holding a plate of cremated sausages, which he was stuffing into his mouth. He shouted and fought against a paramedic, the manager, and a large firefighter, while accusing them of trying to steal his sausages. It may have been comical had it not been so distressing.

That night, the manager had told her they could no longer care for him in his current state; that he needed a residential home. It was then she knew that she would have to put him into care, or care for him herself.

They say dementia can be compared to two bookcases— one containing memories, the most recent at the top, like brand new paperbacks. The lower you peruse on rickety shelves, the tomes are dusty, akin to those you might find in an old bookshop. Oddly, these are the ones you remember when you recall nothing else.

The second bookshelf contains your feelings. A staunch and hard-wearing piece of grained oak furniture, it never wavers. It holds your emotions like a bank vault. It compels you to say; *I don't know who you are, but I know I love you*, with no idea why.

You watch and wait for the inevitable when someone you love has such a disease. Their raft floats on unmoored memories, as they see life continuing around them at the bottom of a lake; one that was once crystal clear but is now polluted and blinding. To watch is torture.

Elizabeth was a nurse; a career she was unsure she would return to – not with her father to care for. She had experienced death and disease. But there was something quintessentially different between caring for strangers and caring for a loved one, especially while the spectre of grief sat on your shoulder like a vulture ready to peck out your eyes. Sometimes, she wished it would.

'I hope Anya picks up some prunes too. I'm constipated,' her father mentioned, his eyes glazing over.

'Did I ever tell you tale of Robert the Bruce?' His father's voice burst rudely into his mind as he passed him his teddy bear. He couldn't take it. His grip on reality was already tenuous.

He shook his head.

'He was buried in my town, boy. One day, I'll take you there. He's a hero, Douglas, a true king of Scotland, just like you, my son.'

His father leaned to kiss his cheek, somehow corporeal once more. His facial hair felt like the horsehair yarn his mother had used in her tailoring, the rolls perfectly arranged next to her sewing machine.

They never visited the King's grave. Now they never would.

He looked down to see the fissure walls lined with black-bound books decorated with gold leaf lettering. Precious, soiled, waterlogged, and mouldering like his psyche.

Once more, the earth quaked, and he realised a book cover had ripped, divided in half, falling forward into the abyss.

He heard nothing more than a rattling from the kitchen.

'He's eaten a week's worth of bread,' Elizabeth snorted.

The knowledge made her chuckle, which developed into hacking laughter, causing her to wonder if it were her losing her mind. Tears streamed down her face as she put the kettle on and searched for some senna. It often amused her how many of her elderly patients' bowels became a frequent topic of conversation. Her father was no different.

'Here's your tea. Drink it down, and then I'll bath you, Dad.'

Her father gave her a queer look like he didn't understand what she was saying.

'But we should be asleep.'

He looked at the clock, which pointed to 5pm.

'No, Dad, it's late afternoon,' Elizabeth said soothingly.

She never ceased to find it strange how life had almost reset itself, how she was the one bathing him and getting him up at night to use the lavatory for fear he might wake in a soggy bed.

'Oh, I wondered why Fiona was on the telly. She's not usually on at night,' he replied, absently feeding Robert the Bruce more treats.

After Dad's bath, they settled down to watch mastermind, which, oddly, her father loved, even though he often didn't get any answers correct. When it had finished, she tucked him into bed in her old dining room. She passed him his battered, old Steiff teddy bear. It had been with him all his life, once hers, now his again.

He caught sight of a cabbage white floating, motionless in his peripheral vision. Those heady days of picnics within the wildflowers of Scotland reminded him of her, the dancing girl in the cheesecloth summer dress, with tiny daisies on the hem, arms spread wide as she spun until her legs gave out and she became a giggling mess. The delightful insects swam through the air above her until they swarmed towards her and covered her.

She was the ledge his foot had finally found, the stability that stopped him from slipping further. When she was born, he had heard a sound when she'd cried, and it had dampened the sound of all others, creating a melody he only heard when she was there. He hummed her tune.

He felt her hand caress his brow. The words he wanted to say wouldn't come. They were alien to him. Instead, she morphed into his mother. She had always looked so much like his mother.

'Mummy,' he said in a small voice, surrounded by blankets, the safety bar pulled up securely on the side of the bed, "I love you."

She kissed his head gently.

'I love you too, Dad.'

The cat stalked below him as he cried out in his sleep.

'Help me!' he begged.

Robert sat back on his haunches, used to the night terrors, licking his paws before padding to the door of the girl. He meowed once to rouse her then lifted his head and sniffed, distracted by the scent of food in the kitchen. Giving up, he strolled back, flicking his tail nonchalantly.

He lifted his head as he heard another shout. Chirping a reply, he decided to answer. It seemed no one else would.

It was these moments that were the killer, those where she had time to think. She knew he felt secure and loved but had no way to articulate it conventionally. She could sit and cry at the injustice of it all. He had once been strong, intelligent, and unyielding against the world. Now, he was reduced to a bag of bones governed by an ineffectual mechanism.

Robert the Bruce had jumped onto her father's stomach with a small chirp as he always did, protectively curling like a serpentine creature within its egg sack. She had thought she would resent having him here. Though it was demanding, she believed she had made the right decision for them both. She knew she would never be able to live with herself if she had sent him to live with strangers.

Her phone rang. It was him again, pressing for an answer.

She placed her hand on her stomach, feeling a small flood of butterflies under her fingertips. It was good to have a secret, though it would have to come out sooner or later. These things always did.

The feline roamed the briars above, inhaling erstwhile scents. Douglas watched Robert's chest undulating with his mouth wide as he breathed in the last of his lifeforce. The disorderly refracted light of a burning lens teemed through his mind, along with a choral serenade of her melody.

He fell, allowing himself to drop.

She needed him to depart so that she could begin.

The Depth of Distance

By Patrick Holloway

Patrick Holloway is a writer of stories and poems. He is the 2021 winner of the Molly Keane Creative Writing Competition, The Allingham Flash Fiction Competition, and the Flash 500 competition. His work has been published by The Stinging Fly, Carve, Overland, The Irish Times, Poetry Ireland Review, The Moth, Southword, among many others. His story, 'Laughing and Turning Away' won second place in the Raymond Carver Short Story Contest. He was highly commended for the Manchester Fiction Prize and shortlisted for numerous other prizes.

The Depth of Distance

There was a sea between us, even when you were home
sitting at the breakfast table.
It gushed. I knew nobody else could see it so I hushed it,
pleading, but it rushed
through the room, taking my Coco Pops, your tea, mum's
low-calorie yoghurt.
I kicked my legs to stay afloat. When you opened the back
door the water
cascaded taking you away down the drive and out of sight.

The shadows of a hundred nights played puppets on the
ceiling.
I could see you on a boat. The penumbra of a feeling I could
not name kneading
my bones until I was all thought. Even though every night I
knew you'd die,
or better yet, I'd kill you, I had to imagine it through. The
circular window,
the water at your neck, your head tilted for the last of
breath, just enough to say,
I love you but it's a lie.

I remember whispering to the waves. Thinking they would
carry you my secrets.
And when they'd crash in spongy sweeps, I'd imagine you
humming,
stroking my hair as I strayed to sleep. When they broke in
such brutal blows
that I'd stand far back, I'd imagine you slamming your
hands on the table,
pleading with me to just do what I was told.

Then you'd be home again and I'd search your face for who you were in my mind.
I'd copycat your walk, the way your mouth would chew. I cursed each day
I didn't grow, hoping each time you returned you'd say, nearly as tall as me, or,
is that still you? Because it never was, still me. I wanted you to see that.

I ran away more than once but nobody noticed. I wanted to be a shell. Driftwood.
A stone for skimming. A buoy. A swell. Anything that would get taken in the sea
and brought to you. I wanted to drown, to know the depths of a well,
to be the echo. To be thrown back from the ocean, unwanted. I wanted to be wanted.
I didn't want to be a boy. I longed to be the people that you spent your time with.
All of them. All at once. I wanted to disappear, for you to never find me.
I dreamed the sea could become a part of me or I am part of the sea. The vastness of it.
The way it takes without attrition, worrying not for what it leaves behind.

And then it took me, years later, far and further still. And when I returned you were aged. And small. I thought I could take you in my hand like a fossil. Study the etches of you, sketch you out on the wall by the back beach, where I had stood, waiting, waiting.
Thought I could wade into the water and from afar call out to you and you'd answer, you'd say, I've been waiting for you to come back to me, all this time, all this time.

The Depth of Distance

Just Off The Boat

By Vivian Oldaker

Vivian has always written stories. Andersen Press published her Young Adult novel "The Killer's Daughter" in 2009. Since then, Vivian has written novels, short stories and plays but sadly none of these has been snapped up by a publisher. Several of her short plays have been performed in front of polite audiences in Salisbury, Plymouth, and Frome. She continues to write, in the hope that someone will read and enjoy.

Just Off The Boat

Respite care, that's what they call it. Spite care, that's what it really is.

I said to David: 'why can't we go back to Broadstairs together, like we always do? But no, that wasn't good enough for my daughter-in-law; it had to be Biarritz for them.'

'Debbie needs a rest, Mother,' David said.

Goodness knows why – she leads the life of Riley.

I call Debbie my daughter-in-law, but in fact, they've never married. Living in sin, we used to call it. Bernard – my late husband – no doubt rolling in his grave. He was religious, respectable. Debbie had twins – not identical, my grandchildren. I haven't seen the girl for years – she's in Canada. Simon, my grandson, owns a bar in Bristol – or possibly Brighton. Or perhaps it's both.

Anyway, David said he and Debbie needed a proper holiday and some guaranteed sunshine; hence, yours truly ends up in The Cedars. It's quite a high-class establishment, but I've no illusions – it's where they put you while they wait for you to die. But at least I'm only here for a fortnight, unlike most of the others.

'Think of it as a little holiday. See how you like it, Mother,' David said.

The residents are a mixed bunch. Nearly all women, as you might expect. Though there's a man next door to me who used to be Mayor of Somewhere; now he just sits, rocking, rubbing away at his knees. He doesn't even know what day of the week it is. To be fair, it's easy to lose track in these circumstances – one day very much like the next.

The food's not bad, though it's never warm enough and all served on cold plates. The carers say it's so we don't burn our mouths. As if I would; I'm eighty-six, not six! They just smile, whatever you say.

The carers treat everyone the same, whether they're away with the fairies – like Mrs. Lemon who keeps saying she was a dancer with the Royal Ballet, (with those legs? I don't think so!) or sensible like me and one or two of the others. Mrs. Fairfax seems a nice woman. She was in banking – or perhaps it was baking, she mumbles a bit. They all do, except the carers, of course. They shout at you like you're deaf and daft.

Not that anyone's cruel. But they don't make allowances. They behave as if we're aliens with a different language and culture. As if we're a separate species to them.

The room's nice enough, I suppose. Magnolia paintwork, blue curtains, and carpet. A picture of Highland cattle on the wall; they look a bit depressed. The manager said I could bring my own furniture, but as it's only for a fortnight, that's a ridiculous notion. He doesn't inspire much confidence – can't be more than thirty-five, hair in a bun. The chest of drawers and the wardrobe look to be made of that MDF stuff – not proper wood anyway. My room has a garden view. Neatly mowed lawns, but they've overdone the rhododendrons.

Not a cedar tree in sight, despite the name of the establishment. I asked someone about that – a girl who comes to clean the room. She's on a gap year. Her name's Tabitha, like a cat. Anyway, she got her phone out. Apparently, cedars are supposed to symbolize eternal life – heaven forbid!

I had a stroke at Christmas – just a little one. Luckily it didn't affect my speech or mobility, but my eyesight's a bit wonky. It happened just as Debbie was serving up the goose. I went face down in the sprouts; they were as hard as musket balls.

In the hospital, I overheard her telling the doctor that my lifestyle was unhealthy. Now, I ask you! If you can't enjoy the odd cigarette and a glass of wine at my age, when can you? Of course, they don't let you smoke in here; I can do without it.

I hope we'll go to Broadstairs again next year. I've always liked it there. My grandson stopped coming with us. It's only natural. Simon's nearly thirty. He almost died when he was two years old – his mother left him unattended in the bath to answer the phone. It was touch and go for a while. Maybe the trauma was what turned him homosexual. But they say they're born that way, so perhaps not. There's nothing like that on our side, but Debbie's family are all very theatrical.

Of course, if it hadn't been for the bath overflowing and bringing down the ceiling in the kitchen, I might have been able to stay at home. It really wasn't my fault, despite what Debbie said. I always take showers – much more hygienic. It must have been Mary. She's the so-called cleaner.

I told Debbie, 'When you pay peanuts, you get monkeys.'

She accused me of being a racist! I told her, it's a well-known expression and Mary's race has nothing to do with it. Besides, she's from the Philippines and they don't count as black, do they? Debbie always makes mountains out of molehills.

I said to her, 'be thankful for small mercies - at least there was no-one in the bath when it happened.'

If eye-rolling were an Olympic sport, Debbie would win the gold medal every time. They didn't ask me to go to France with them, but I wouldn't have gone anyway. I don't care for frogs' legs and snails.

Yesterday, we had Music and Memory. They started off with 'It's a Long Way to Tipperary.' Really! How old do they think we are? That's a First World War song. There's a few here in their nineties and a couple of centenarians, but most of us were children when the Second War kicked off. Wing Commander Thomas reckons he was in Bomber Command, but he looks younger than me, so he can't have been. He's obviously a sandwich short.

I've got a Memory Book. One of the carers – the African one – helped me fill it in. I told her there was no point, that I was only here for respite, but she just laughed and said we might as well get it done anyway.

She had some schoolchildren with her – they wanted to know all about my life, though one kept getting her phone out of her pocket when she thought no-one was looking to check her Facebook.

'Do you prefer Mrs. Baron or Elizabeth?' the carer asked.

I couldn't get what she meant for a moment – just for a moment mind – and she said to the schoolchildren, 'some of them can be a bit slow to understand.' Like I was a foreigner just off the boat.

I said, 'I comprehend your meaning perfectly well, thank you. And I'll be pleased if you'll address me as Mrs. Baron.'

One of the schoolgirls giggled.

'And what's your name?' I asked her.

'Cheyenne' she said.

Heavens to Betsy! 'Cheyenne like a Red Indian?' I said.

The carer chips in: 'We say 'Native American' or 'First Nation' nowadays, Mrs. Baron.'

Though she had the smile wiped off her face when Cheyenne said no, it was after a German Shepherd her mother once owned. We got talking about dogs then. I know dogs. I used to judge them in the Show Ring.

At least the African carer asked me about my name; most of them just call me 'Liz.' I've never been Liz, not even as a child. Elizabeth like the Queen and the Queen's Mother. Someone once said I had a look of Princess Margaret; it

may have been my husband. In here, when they call me
'Liz,' I don't respond. They have to learn.

I told the African carer and the children about my
life – well, the edited highlights anyway. Childhood in
Hampshire, no bombs or bullets to speak of. Good at
school; the best handwriting in my class.

I worked for Mr. Baron; he was a shoe importer; I was
his secretary – I had to explain to the children what that
entailed. I suppose secretaries are more-or-less obsolete
nowadays, what with computers.

I married Mr. Baron's brother; we had David soon after.
All the shoes I could want, lovely Italian leather. I kept
house, cooked. I was the first one in our circle to make
Spaghetti Bolognese. Joined the Townswomen's Guild.
(I had to explain that one too.) Very active in the Drama
Group – I was Madam Arcati in Blithe Spirit. The drama
critic on the local paper said he'd never seen a theatrical
performance like it. Widowed at forty-two. After Bernard
died there were my pugs – I was a highly-regarded breeder,
then a judge.

The schoolchildren struck me as a little lacking in brains.
They didn't seem to understand half of what I said, I
might just as well have been speaking Swahili. The world's
vastly changed since I was their age of course. Cheyenne
had pierced ears – that would have been considered very
lower class and common when I was a girl. Gypsies did
it. Cheyenne seemed offended – I don't know why; I was
only telling the truth. The African explained that political
correctness was often poorly understood by people of my
age. Political poppycock!

After they'd all cleared off, I got out my magnifying glass
and took a look at my memory book. She'd written that I
used to breed bugs; I ask you! Is she deaf or just plain daft?

I wandered along to the upstairs lounge yesterday. A few

magazines lying about, all full of word searches and those – what are they called? Pseudo-queues – or some such; Japanese. In my day, we didn't like the Japanese. Now, their puzzles are supposed to keep our brains active. Life nowadays the big puzzle. The whole world a puzzle. What's it all about, Alfie?

I used to quite like COSMOPOLITAN, even though it was full of sex. NOVA was another one – long gone. I saw Mrs. Lemon reading a Woman's Own. She was holding it upside down.

The African carer – her name's Brenda – says she's got some big print books I might like. I don't much care for fiction nowadays. Life isn't all happily-ever-after, and it's no good writers pretending otherwise.

I wonder how David and Debbie are getting on in wherever it is. Somewhere in France. I suppose she could be worse, Debbie. My neighbours' daughter-in-law ended up in prison for fraud. You don't expect that sort of thing in our cul-de-sac.

Debbie and I have never seen eye-to-eye. No sooner had they moved in with me than she started on what she called 'improvements'.

Perfectly good carpets in the skip and the gas cooker thrown over for an Aga. Then, she decided we should properly pool our resources and buy somewhere bigger with a separate granny flat for me. It was my resources, not theirs. They had no resources.

David never amounted to much; a deputy head was the best he could manage.

Dear old Broadstairs. Debbie makes such a fuss about everything. Last year, she insisted on inviting all these people to lunch with us while we were there. All I did was move the canapés and the sandwiches out of the fridge to the table outside, so they had a chance to acclimatise before the guests arrived. I was trying to help. It was the day I lost my stockings, and someone had put my shoes in the oven.

I had a lot on my mind. How was I to know the dog was out there? Of course, what he left, the seagulls had. It's Debbie's own fault for getting a Labrador – everyone knows how greedy they are. She should have gone in for a Cavalier, like I wanted. Of course, David sided with her; he always does. They say daughters are more loving, more considerate, than sons.

That Mrs. Fairfax – the baker or the banker – was kicking off at lunch today. Just because Ramesh poured her too much gravy – well, he hasn't been trained in it. Ma Fairfax started on about bloody immigrants - fucking ignorant immigrants was what she actually said – appalling language!

I told her, 'You're the one who's ignorant. I feel sorry for them – countries destroyed by war or famine, risking their lives in leaky boats, arriving here, cold, hungry, frightened, confused, entrusting their lives to some man. Having to suffer abuse from stupid people like you.'

She threw a bread roll at me.

Ramesh isn't a carer; he's a doctor; Doctor Ramesh. He was only trying to help out; like me with the canapés in Broadstairs. Not that Doctor Ramesh came over in a boat. He lives in Boscombe – or possibly Branksome. Very handsome.

David will be fetching me out of here soon. I want to be ready. It seems a long time they've been gone.

I was sitting in the downstairs lounge yesterday, some nonsense on the telly, when my grandson popped in with his boyfriend – that's how he introduced him; straight out with it.

'Granny, this is my boyfriend, Buttons.'

That can't have been his name, surely?

The so-called boyfriend was bald and fifty if he was a day; boyfriend indeed! My grandson – I'm almost sure his name is Simon – said his mum and dad had been back a while, but that can't be right, can it? He also said they'd been in to see me, but they jolly well hadn't. I'd have remembered that.

After they'd gone, Fatty Fairfax started on, 'your grandson's a nancy-boy then?'

Brenda said to take no notice, but Fatty Fairfax said she could tell I was ashamed – bloody nerve! Bloody fucking nerve!

I said Simon wasn't a nancy-boy; he was gay, and I wasn't in the least bit ashamed. Simon's my pride and joy. It's just that I think he could do better.

'It's the Circle of Life and the something, something...' I wish we sang songs like that at Saturday Singalong. Elton John. He's gay too. Far too old for my Simon, though, which is a shame as he's very rich and has a lovely voice. The circle of life, going round and round and round. Stop the world, I want to get off.

I asked Brenda if Doctor Ramesh has a boyfriend. She laughed and laughed. I'll ask him myself if I get the chance.

'I wish I was, Homeward Bound. Home, where the something takes me.' Simon and Garfunkel – they were nice. Not gay. Simon was quite the opposite, something of a swordsman by all accounts.

'A son is a son till he takes a wife, a daughter's a daughter the rest of her life.' I had a daughter – we called her Jennifer. Dear little thing, beautiful brown eyes. A sister for David, all the way from Zanzibar. When we lost her to measles, Bernard's view was least said soonest mended. It was the only time I ever shouted at him. 'Screaming like a fishwife,' his mother said. She never liked me because I wasn't Jewish. I closed myself right down for a while after Jennie died. I should have had counseling, really, but it hadn't been invented then.

I had a little adventure yesterday. We're not really allowed to go out on our own in case we've forgotten how to cross the road or have a fall or do what Mrs. Lemon did once, which was nip into Waitrose and stuff avocados into her unmentionables. They were ready-to-eat ones too, such a waste.

Anyway, it was a lovely day and I fancied an outing. This is supposed to be a home, not a Detention Centre, so, I sneaked out after the chiropodist. I don't have her, so she doesn't know me.

I walked down to the river to feed the ducks – only, there weren't any, so I sat on a bench for a bit and watched the world go by. They found me eventually, which was probably just as well because, by then, it was getting a bit chilly, and I wasn't quite sure of the way back.

'I didn't take you for a wanderer,' The African carer said. I think her name's Brenda. 'I can see I'm going to have to keep my eye on you.'

'Whatevs,' I said. It's something I learned from Cheyenne. It's best to know the modern lingo if you want to survive in this world.

I had a daughter. What was her name? I should be able to remember that. My head's getting awfully full of holes.

I asked Wotsername – Brenda – if she was from Zanzibar, but it turns out she's from Devizes.

It's raining outside, puddles in the driveway, Brenda keeps telling me to take off my coat. She says I'm not going anywhere. Perhaps David's planning to collect me after lunch; it's fish pie today. Quite nice, but they serve it too hot.

They keep changing the view from my bedroom window. Is it a test? Do they think I won't notice? Today I can see the harbour. I'm watching them landing the lobster pots and all the little boats are hurrying in. There may be a storm coming.

I'm spending more time in my room lately. This house is confusing. It's easy to get lost. Brenda said I should come downstairs and join the others this afternoon. A man's coming to show us his owls.

I said to her, 'What do I want with owls at my time of life?'

I'm quite happy watching the goings on in the marketplace from my window.

I hope David gets a move on with the car to collect me. I'm all ready to go. If he doesn't get here soon, I'll ask Wotsername to phone him, ask him to hurry up. I feel like an alien, just off the boat, such a long way from home. I really don't belong here – but then again, who does?

The Stars Are Falling

By Sophie Evans

Sophie Evans is a 22-year-old writer from Bournemouth, England. Growing up with a twin sister, her work often centers around the themes of sisterhood and family relationships. She has enjoyed writing fiction for most of her life, and sometimes dabbles in poetry.

The Stars Are Falling

and we lie here watching it happen,
this astral Armageddon.

The constellations crumble piece by piece,
Andromeda, Cassiopeia, Ursas Minor and Major,
disintegrate into nothingness before our eyes.

The moon's crescent smile spits
specks of light down on us, and she grins
as though it is the greatest gift she should give.

Like pieces of glowing confetti,
the stars twirl and flutter towards the Earth, leaving
the endless night a pool of midnight ink; in this moment
if the world were to tip upside down,
we'd drown in it.

Catch one for me, you whisper
and I stretch my hands to the heavens,
waiting, hoping, aching for
a star to descend in our direction. And then

minutes later, we spot one plummeting towards us.
You jump up, shouting *over there over there* and
I run towards the light, leap into the air,
and as my fist closes around it,
the damned thing burns a hole
through my palm and
falls to its final resting place
at our feet.

The night air stinks of my singed skin
and upon further inspection we discover
that the star I had tried to catch
was, in fact,
the Sun.

Blackberry Picking

By Brigitte de Valk

Brigitte de Valk is the winner of the Cúirt New Writing Prize 2020 (adjudicated by Claire-Louise Bennett) and the Royal Holloway Art Writing Competition. She was awarded second place in the Benedict Kiely Short Story Competition and was longlisted for The Alpine Fellowship Writing Prize 2020. Her entry to the Bournemouth Writing Prize 2021 was selected for publication. Brigitte's short fiction is also published by Happy London Press and Reflex Press.

Blackberry Picking

The silk chiffon of summer had fallen away. Autumn was revealed, nude and cold. There was a sense of relief. The gaiety of the previous season was over, and the fields of the countryside were saturated in subtle brown hues. It was October. The earth could finally breathe.

Belle shivered. She could feel the uneven texture of the ground beneath her boots. Cows had trodden along the path when the soil had been wet, and their hooves had left deep groove marks. There was a metallic quality to the air, like the must of old copper pennies found at the back of a drawer.

A carrier bag full of empty tin cans rustled and clinked as Belle walked. It formed a musical accompaniment to each long stride she took. She glanced up as she entered a new field. The sky was a stark pale grey, with muscular clouds that bulged, almost touching the ground in the far distance. Smoke, from a bonfire, fled into the sky and quickly disappeared. Dead branches and shrubberies were being burnt. Belle paused and took a deep breath. Her heartbeat was uneven. The thought of death was too prescient.

'Blackberries,' Belle murmured.

She cleared her throat. An image of Seamus Heaney bloomed in her mind. She imagined the gentle gravitas of his voice as he recited poetry. There was a dark warmth to his eyes. Ever since her father died, Belle had sought the paternal elsewhere. She crouched down and placed her palm against dry earth. She crumbled a little soil between her fingertips. Her father had never looked at her directly when he spoke. His gaze flitted about the room, alighting nervously here and there. His pupils were trapped blackbirds, encircled by a hazel ring.

Belle stood. She redid the top button of her coat. The muscles in her legs ached quietly; she had been walking for hours. There were pink marks on her hands from where the plastic handle of the bag had cut. She thought of the way her father had talked to her, through gesticulation, mostly, and subtle facial movements. He hummed a little, and when he did speak, his voice was soothing and rough, like the texture of recently chopped wood. Communication solely through words seemed a bereft approach to language. Besides, Belle had never prioritised sentences strung beautifully together. She was averse to the hierarchy of fluid prose. She preferred the dark crackle of the fire at night, or the sound of her heart, beating dimly within her constricted chest.

There was a dull glamour to the sky now. A touch of gold had appeared on the horizon. Belle began to walk, her pace a little quicker. Her tastes were changing. She was turning to poetry to fill the silence her father had left. Perhaps Heaney was a good place for her to start. He seemed to invite certain cadences to his words, like underground rivers, flowing invisibly. Belle surveyed the hedgerows. She could spy the black fruit she was after, but there was an adamant, almost superstitious, spark in her that led her further onward to a particular grove she wanted to pluck from. There was an elusive quality to Heaney, as with her father. Nature had whispered intimate secrets into their ears as they slept.

Belle pushed open the cold iron of a gate. It groaned in lament. She re-bolted it, a slight tremor to her fingers – they were growing numb. Her knuckles protruded, a harsh-red, like small mountains against the rest of her skin.

Belle straightened and turned around. She had arrived; this was the field. It was deserted. The soil had been tilled into neat rows that stretched endlessly away. She neared the bramble hedges where clots of dark fruit clung to their branches. A smile passed over Belle's face, like sunlight glancing through a thick cloudscape. Blackberries in autumn were latecomers to a dying party. They were the last piquant sting before the season shriveled into a colder, drab version of itself.

Belle's hand reached forward, and her fingertips clumsily picked a cluster of berries. She dropped them soundlessly into a tin. She was too cold to feel the pinpricks of the thorns. Again, she navigated the intricate web of branches and drew forth black, edible gold. The tins soon filled.

A tear threatened to spill at the edge of her eye. She blinked it away. The noise of cows lowing could be heard in a memory that surfaced. It coupled with the opaque silhouette of her father, walking in the distance, his shoulders stooped. Belle pressed her lips together. She concentrated on the inky gloss of the berries; anticipation of their sharp flavour drummed in the air.

Coal dust lingered on Belle's palms. The scrape of a shovel ceased, the iron bucket was full enough. Belle leant the shovel against the side of the stone shed and clapped her hands together, trying to dislodge the dirt. The scent of mould filled her nostrils. It was peaceful here. The shed felt like a go-between, between the exterior and the interior world. The wild unknowability of nature was mirrored in the crevices and shadows of its walls. It possessed an inherent discomfort and cold; with its fine lines of web intricately wrought in all four corners. And yet, Belle straightened and wrapped her fingers around the handle of the bucket, the shed pertained a gentle hush, that could not exist outside. She heard each faint breath she took, shallow yet regular.

Belle paused on her route back to the kitchen. Night burgeoned swiftly, and she inhaled the refreshing dark of the air, fertile as soil. Vines viciously ribboned themselves through the garden. Discarded tools were vague outlines as water dripped sedately into a metal dish. It provided an iron echo.

This was once her father's favourite time of day. He felt vitalised by the shadowed beauty of nocturnality, the pressure of expectation fell from his narrow frame. He would call his daughter into the living room, and they would sit together with the windows wide open, even in winter. Belle would be wrapped in a blanket, while her father simply wore his long coat. They kept an oath of silence and listened to the indistinct noise of night-time.

The kitchen bled a mellow rectangle of gold. Belle entered and closed the door behind her. She carefully stepped out of her boots and placed the coal bucket on the tiles. She rinsed her hands in the sink, turning the water dark and then clear. Mounds of blackberries littered the counter tops, they sat in saucepans and colanders, bowls, and mugs. The berries gleamed with water droplets; they were irresistible, brain-like, thorned.

Belle placed a berry in the palm of her hand. She rolled it around with the tip of her forefinger, and then let it drop into the basin of the sink. Its skin felt smooth, as though polished with nature's sweat. Heaney had watched his blackberry riches disintegrate into a rat-grey fungus. As a boy, he had experienced a hot flush of disappointment. The concept of beauty's death lingered at the back of his throat as he read his poems aloud. His words caught on this grief, like a match being struck, providing a guttural acknowledgement of nature's brutality.

Belle flicked off the kitchen lights.

The white of the hospital pillow drained what little colour remained in her father's face. His eyelids twitched haphazardly. The tangle of his wrinkles, deeply etched,

seemed to rebel against the neat order of the room. Belle
had stood by the window, her elbow on the sill, watching
the curtains flutter. They were made of delicate gauze. Her
father was fading away. She could feel this somehow, and
her only thoughts were of regret. He shouldn't die here.
His last breath should take place outside. Her fingers tried
to pry open the window, but it was locked. A faint scent of
disinfectant edged around the corners of the room.

Burgundy carnations were arranged untidily in a vase.
Belle avoided looking at them. Their petals reminded her of
dried blood.

The corridor echoed with footsteps, and frustration
fluttered in her chest, but then, calmed, like leaves settling
on the ground. Her father's hand rested on his chest. It was
a limp, pale thing, moving up and down with the rhythm of
his weak diaphragm. She memorised its every contour and
freckle until her vision grew blurred.

Belle's childhood bedroom rippled with shadows as she
slipped under the bedcovers. The sheets were cold and
soothing. An aged bear lay next to her pillow; her eyes
remained open. The mattress creaked a little.

There was an elegiac quality to the blackberries, who
remained silent downstairs, dressed in mourning. Words
failed. Or at least they had at the funeral. Belle's throat
had become choked with lacklustre words. She had
stood at the church pulpit, looking down at the oval faces
that stared back at her, and she couldn't utter a thing.
Eventually, someone led her down and sat her on a wooden
pew. Ringing had filled her ears. Her father's casket was
unadorned.

Belle closed her eyes. Dreams began to orientate
themselves around her last conscious thoughts. Soon,
the night deepened into something electric. Belle stood
barefoot on a barren field. She was painting with blackberry

juice: a naked body formed on a large canvas. It was a silhouette she was familiar with. Belle peered at it closely, and goosepimples formed along her shoulders. She realised the canvas was a mirror. She was nude. The outline in the glass could no longer contain the feeling that broiled in her veins. It began to merge with the clouds reflected in the background. Belle stepped forward.

She awoke with a gasp. After a moment, she turned over and fell into a quieter sleep.

Coffee filled her mouth. The charcoal aftereffects of dawn laced themselves across the sky while Belle sat on the kitchen step; her palms warmed by the mug. A few brown sparrows rustled in a tall tree. Heaney's voice resounded quietly from a speaker. It filled her with a calm acceptance. His poems perfectly fit the wooden grooves of her memories, and the knots that formed where branches had once been. Morning broke gently on the horizon.

She wore her father's long coat, draped over her shoulders.

Walking With William Butler

By Jennifer Armstrong

Jennifer is a writer from the West of Ireland, now living in London. She is due to complete the MA in Creative Writing at UEA in the year 22-23. Her contact email is jenniferarm92@gmail.com

Walking With William Butler

Old Willie takes my hand and walks me slowly up the side of Benbulben. Steep and gravelly, there is danger lurking with every step and misstep. Old Willie is long dead and has no fear of what lays beneath or ahead. He sleeps amongst the lambs that graze, and the warrior's bones that have been ground down and trampled on decade after decade. I have a life still to live. I dig my heels deeper into the soil, praying for grip.

He wants to walk up the northern rim, the angle almost vertical straight into the sky. I convince him to take the south side, which meanders more softly into the clouds.

'I want to show you something', he says, 'while the day is still glorious with sunshine.'

All the while, there is a ringing in my ear. The sound of someone singing in the distance. The melancholy chanting of bleak hymns and doleful refrains.

When I look around, I cannot see another soul. I reckon it must be just Old Willie, whispering ditties as usual under his breath. I hear it still as we pass through the fields, which remain wet with dew even though the morning has left. Willie instructs me to reach down and move my fingers through the grass.

'The ground here never fully dries', he tells me. 'There is a certain texture brought down by the clouds into the atmosphere, which keeps the air moist and the soil damp.'

Willie does not mention the rain, pouring relentlessly from the heavens.

Willie is old and grey and full of sleep. Despite his eagerness, he can go no quicker than a lame pup. I feel slow myself because, even though the weather is beginning to turn, the wind is harsh at this height, and cuts through the skin on my cheeks. It has grown thinner as I have aged and now seems almost translucent.

I am made even more cautious by the unfamiliar ground beneath my feet. It feels different to the dependable soil in the graveyard below, which is made up mostly of decaying bodies and organic matter. The dirt here seems to be undisturbed for centuries, interrupted only with the footprints of the sheep and cattle that roam the fields and guard the mountain.

I have been visiting my dead mother, who sleeps in the ground beside Willie, next to the church and the café where they sell claddagh rings and serve quiche. She has been dead for years but lately it feels as though she has been leaving me slowly, all over again. Without my consent, corners of my mind replay her last moments. It is worst in the mornings when I am still half dreaming – I feel the grip of her fingers around mine tighten and relax. A steady beat, playing out some familiar tune.

Now, I feel Willie's wrinkled hand wrapped around my own, which he squeezes tight when we come upon an unsteady piece of ground. He is whistling an old song and reciting bits of poems.

'I will arise and go now; go to Inisbofin.'

Willie is not well, retreating further by the minute into madness. Verse jumbles in his head, which he splutters out in meaningless rhymes. He is convinced "the golden apples" are of Ballymun. He picks a dandelion that has gone to seed and blows the feathery strands into the air. He goes on, recalling his aimless decades on these hills, "wandering lonely as a cloud".

'That's not even yours', I protest, but he ignores me.

He drives onwards until we reach a treacherous stony

path where we must fall to our hands and knees to creep up slowly like lost dogs.

As we inch forward, he asks about my sadness, and I explain about my mother and how I can feel her around me all the time. Sometimes, I am boiling the kettle in the morning or replacing the toilet paper with fresh roll and the remembering that she is gone hits me anew. Then, it is like the day she died all over again, and I feel a burning pain searing through my chest and my stomach collapsing. Her laugh was infectious, and without her, I have fallen out of the habit. For a while, grief felt like a muscle I had strengthened. But lately, my whole-body aches with stiffness, as though every limb has atrophied, and I just want to rest.

Willie offers me a moth-eaten handkerchief from his pocket. He tries to change the subject, reminding me of the beauty of the landscape and the wonderful assault on our senses even now as we climb. The wet grass under our feet and the cold air on our skin, the smell of the moss and the faint whisper on our tongues of salt from the sea. It is hard to take Willie seriously, given his mud-stained green lapels and perspective on life, which has been so altered by his many decades in the afterlife.

'The world has indeed "changed utterly",' Willie goes on, 'and yet, this lovely mound of limestone has not moved nor bent in millions of years. The fossils and bones of the dead sea creatures are still preserved like magic, sewn into these layers of sedimentation.' Willie smiles as he puts his hand down to touch the porous stone. 'Hard and unwavering even in the harshest wind.'

I suddenly hear it again despite Willie's tiresome gibberish – the distant voices reciting prayers – but this time, it is more like a choir, singing in a minor key.

We soon come upon a field of lambs, stumbling around

like drunkards. Then, further up the ones born two days ahead, leaping about like children in a playground.

'But you once wrote this was all due to end and be destroyed', I press him after we have walked a while in silence. 'You wrote "the Centre cannot hold", "things fall apart", "the Second Coming was upon us"?'

'Did I really?' Willie looks at me bemused. 'Bah, what do I know.' He pats the head of a rogue lamb who has strayed from its mother – 'we tell ourselves stories in order to live.'

'That's Joan Didion's line', I object.

'Ah well, she nicked one of mine too.'

A farmer begins to follow us and his lambs, which have strayed, chasing them over the low stone wall where he falls and shouts obscenities. We run until we are far away from his land, though it is indistinguishable from the rest and still full of the same soil and bones. We stop to take a rest, to look out over Sligo town, which appears just a cluster of tiny shacks.

Willie points to a gathering of people on the north side of town, near the turn for the hospital. I tell Willie it is Connolly's pub, where they are serving takeaway pints and drams of whiskey. He licks his lips and slowly moves his finger westward to the tall grey statue outside the Ulster Bank.

'It's you', I tell him.

He says nothing, but straightens his back before we move on, fixing his tie and brushing the dirt from his trousers. We turn to the ocean then, to gaze across the piece of land jutting out into the sea – the last stop before New York, my mother used to say.

I tell him about his summer home at Elsinore in Rosses Point village, and how it sits now just as abandoned blocks of stone, covered in cages to keep the strangers out, a piece of history being let wear and run down to ruins. Once more, the lines on his brow deepen.

'Tear it down,' he eventually utters with a dismissive wave of the hand, ' 'tis nothing but a pile of old stones.'

'Now honestly, we must hurry on,' he urges, 'we are already late.'

Finally, we reach the summit and sit down for a long rest before we begin to stroll across the flat top of the mountain. My head begins to whir with the altitude, and my stomach feels light, like I am riding a rollercoaster of endless loops.

Willie looks across at Knocknarea and poses as though firing an arrow in the direction of Maeve, standing upright in her tomb prepared eternally for duel. He lends her a graceful bow, conceding before beginning.

'I do not have the strength to take on the Queen', he smiles, 'she has centuries on me.'

I begin to stumble, low on sugar and mouth dry. I nearly trip over the loose stones below into a marshy pool full of spawn. I am struggling to keep up with Willie's nonsense, which is doing nothing to alleviate the heavy pressure mounting in my chest and the dense air stifling my lungs.

But still, he goes on.

'All in all, Sligo looks grand,' he nods as he purveys the scene, 'it still seems to be nestled safely away between the two auld peaks. The Garvogue as well, I can see now, continues to gush into the salty water of the bay, full of swans and mallards fighting for bread.'

'Longer days are on the horizon', he muses as he clasps his hands behind his back and motions me onwards. 'Look there, the grounds of Lissadell House covered in layers of bluebells, almost the colour of a violent indigo tide rushing into the dunes, distinct only from the sea by their scent, which wafts across to the sailors, floating on the waves by the Lower Rosses.'

I look across in amazement. The bluebells had not been there days before, but now when I turn my head, it is all I can see; fields of them flooding into the Hazelwood. Willie walks on as I pinch the skin around my wrist to try and get the blood flowing again to the tips of my fingers, blue with cold and dry against my palms. Soon, we have walked the entire length of the tabletop mountain. Below us stretching down is the curved edge of the cliff, which from Sligo town looks like the yawning tongue of a tired collie.

Willie asks me to sit next to him and dangle my feet over the drop that falls almost 2000 feet. I step backwards, but still, he beckons me forward and tells me to look to the left to Sligo town; glistening now that the sun is out. Straight ahead, the sea is as calm as glass, but no doubt as cold as Christmas morning. He is unrelenting in his efforts until, finally, I succumb, sitting on the stony ground to his left, curling my legs up under my arms.

'It is quite a sight, isn't it?', Willie exclaims.

I am about to beg him to shut up, but when I turn, he has laid straight back and is already dosing, cheeks angling up towards the sky.

Instead, I am startled by the eyes of my mother, sitting on his right-hand side gazing back at me. I wonder what she is doing here, because I am sure I watched her myself, being lowered into the ground at the bottom of this hill. She wakes up Willie and says we must get ready.

'We are already running late,' she says.

She is entirely familiar, even the smell of her perfume and talc floats towards me with the breeze. Her eyes are the same deep shade of blue that, in the natural light of the sun, go green around the rim. I want to stand up and make my way back down the south side, but my legs feel heavy and hard like the stones below.

My mother takes my hand in hers and I can suddenly sense it then, the feeling of heavy soil closing in around my body. I am overcome with satisfaction, and the comforting feeling of the soft satin cushion which is grazing the skin of my neck. I feel the density of the ground, which surrounds me, down by the church, lying side by side with my mother and Willie, making acquaintances with dead souls and the vegetation of the Spring. I notice a beautiful lightness in my bowels and no longer feel an ounce of hunger. My mother and Willie gaze out towards the sea before both turning slowly to face me, expressions calm and expectant. I realize then why we have come all this way.

Old Willie gets up and walks around so he is on my left and I am sat between them both, my fingers locked tightly into theirs. We glance down into the plummeting bottom below and I close my eyes in fear, but somehow, I can still see perfectly – the town and beaches and mountains laid out before me. We begin to maneuver our bums gently over the edge, like cautious children on a playground slide. For an instant, I want to scramble back inwards, away from the cliff and the steep drop as something reminiscent of a heart pounds in my chest. But it is much too late for that now. The beating heart has left me, and inside I am only air. When I look down, I see we are floating weightless by the ledge, and then we are not floating at all.

As we go down, my skin – a moment ago cold and thin – begins to grow full of heat. It becomes covered in the creamy particles of the low hanging clouds. Somehow, the sharp edges of the stones and deep grooves in the rock feel like duck feathers on my bum. We go so fast the breeze takes the breath from my lungs, and even then, I can only laugh as the cold wind is blurring my vision. I see nothing but a haze of colours, mostly green and blue. Some yellow from the flowers and grey from the houses, still brimming with life.

I let go of Willie's hand and gather bunches of daffodils, which flood the fields we pass. At the bottom, I am still holding my mother's hand, but she is lying backwards in the grass facing the sky, smiling madly at the sun.

'Soon, they will be gone,' Willie says, glancing at the daffodils in my hand, which have already begun to wilt, 'because I'm afraid Spring has lasted long enough.' He brushes the dirt from his jacket as he begins to stroll back up towards the summit, 'but then, of course, the summer will come, and the raspberries bushes will begin to bear fruit which will be sour and sweet and burst on your tongue.'

'People will rob them from the fields, and the pink will stain their lips and teeth as though they have all been mad with kissing, like teenagers in love.' My mother gives a hearty laugh that I can feel echo deep down in my belly.

I do not know how long we spent falling, it might have been forever – I might still be falling now.

Love Apples

By Liz Houchin

Liz Houchin lives in Dublin. She holds an MA in Creative Writing from University College Dublin. 'Anatomy of a Honey girl,' her first chapbook was published in 2021. She was recently awarded a literature bursary from the Arts Council of Ireland. Her work has appeared in Banshee, Journal.ie, RTE, and has been shortlisted in competitions including the Fish, Bridport, Irish Novel Fair and Fool for Poetry prizes.

Love Apples

Three days after Christmas, in a semi-detached house in Dublin, Barbara laid to rest the carcass of her twenty-third turkey. This was how she measured the passing of time, a much more respectable number than her age. Both her children had brought friends home from college who had nowhere else to be, and she was grateful for their animation and their appetites. They were now gone to drink in the New Year in some unsuspecting country house. Her husband had nipped to the office to check on things, so she finally had the place to herself. She worked from home as a literary agent and spent the morning responding to emails from her authors—a mix of good wishes and existential despair—and over lunch she ordered tomato seeds: *Gardener's Delight, Sungold* and a new black tomato, *Indigo Rose,* because you only live once.

Her love of tomatoes began on a hot July afternoon fifty years previously when her mother, on seeing the shadow of the health visitor at the door, shoved a carton of tomatoes in front of her as she sat on the grass in nothing but a pair of frilly pants. The health visitor had come to see Barbara's baby brother, who had spent his first weeks in an incubator. As she was packing away the tools of her trade, she looked over from the kitchen chair that was moonlighting as garden furniture.

'Well, you'll never need to worry about her appetite,' she said.

Her mother followed her gaze to the orange rivulet running down Barbara's chubby torso and the empty carton resting on her head of blonde curls. For the rest of the summer, anytime she was asked what she would like to eat, Barbara would simply say 'meat and mat,' translated as ham and tomatoes. Barbara had eaten them almost every day of her life.

Six weeks later, on Valentine's Day, Barbara stood in her ancient greenhouse and turned on the AM/FM radio that still had its original batteries and never minded a dusting of compost or a splash from a watering can. The midmorning presenter was reading out the winning entry to a love poem competition, the subject seemingly a labradoodle named Billy. It was quite touching really.

Barbara got to work sowing her tomato seeds in the same little pots as last year. It was her favourite gardening job; the promise of new life and better weather. She knew they would germinate, as sure as she knew the authors who would turn in their manuscript before the deadline and the ones who would put all their creative energy into excuses and lies, some of which were exceptionally good and could easily have been turned into flash fiction or perhaps a haiku. February was holding on to winter with both hands, and a fierce westerly rattled the fragile aluminium frame that threatened to simply crash to the ground one of these days. Two of the windows were held together with packing tape. Just as she was watering the pots, her husband appeared and coaxed the door open wide enough to pass through a shocking pink orchid.

'Happy Valentine's Day!' he said, flushed.

'Well thank you, this is a surprise,' she put down her watering can and leaned over for a kiss, careful to keep her hands away from his suit.

'I was in the shops and thought you'd like it.'

'You went to a shop? Well there's a first time for everything. I'll just finish up here and get us some lunch. You can tell me all about your adventures in retail.'

'Actually, I've to run back to the office, but I'll be home

for dinner.'

She tore the heart printed cellophane from around the plant and watched him sprint away. While the colour of the flower was mildly offensive, she was grateful for his sudden rush of blood to the head. She felt bad that she hadn't bought him anything, but he valued a good meal above most things. She looked forward to a steak dinner and a glass of wine, but by the time he came home his mood had changed and when she thanked him again for the orchid, he seemed embarrassed, almost like it had been a lapse of judgement that he hoped everyone would have the decency to forget.

A month later, she decamped to the greenhouse on a Saturday morning to transplant the seedlings into bigger pots. Holding one of the first true leaves between her fingers she used an old pencil to lift the white thready roots from the soil and move them to their second home where they would have room to spread out and support five feet of vines. She repeated this action over and over while reading a draft of her favourite author's new novel, covering it in brown thumbprints. It was getting harder to sell books written by people who remembered life before the Internet but this one would be difficult to ignore. She hoped it would remind people that, like the mock orange she had planted beside the front door, some of the most beautiful flowers bloomed only on old wood.

Pausing to turn the page, she noticed her husband on his phone in the shed at the end of the garden. There was no reason for him to be in there and he seemed quite agitated, pacing about as much as anyone could pace in a shed. Their shed was a damp gloomy place where DIY dreams went to die, so Barbara kept her gardening tools in the greenhouse. He must have been aware that she could see him, so that evening she asked him if everything was alright.

'I saw you on your phone in the shed.'

'Yes, yes, just work, trying to persuade HR to bend the rules for a new hire.'

'Right. I thought it was something more dramatic.'

'Colonel Mustard in the shed with a screwdriver. Not everything's a murder mystery you know.'

'I was thinking more along the lines of a suburban thriller—disguised as a middle-aged accountant, a secret agent takes down the head of the residents' association who is, of course, a war criminal.'

'Nothing that exciting I'm afraid. Anyway, I'm going to pick up some notes from the office that I should review before Monday. Need anything?'

On the second Sunday in April, it was warm enough to have lunch in the garden. Barbara brushed down two garden seats for the first time that year and stole a cushion from the kitchen to insulate her behind from the damp. Nothing signaled summer's approach like eating outside. Pointing out new tulips she had planted the previous autumn, or planning a holiday, they would sit and chat and laugh. But not this time. Her husband was just back from a two-day business trip, and all she felt was a tightness in her chest that had been quietly building for weeks. She had considered a rare visit to the GP, but a phone call the previous day had diagnosed the problem and it was time to share. She put down her fork.

'So, when are you going to tell me?'

'Sorry?'

'Yes, you should be, but I doubt you are.'

'What?' he kept his focus on his plate.

'The estate agent called with some good news while you were away. He has someone on his books who is interested in viewing our house. I thanked him warmly. He must have assumed that the house was in both our names and that I knew it was going on the market.' She picked up her fork and returned to her quiche. Her heart was now bouncing off her ribcage.

'Oh Barbara, I was just making enquiries,' he said, 'I was going to talk to you first, but I was waiting for the right time.' He reached out his hand and placed it over hers.

'It's all just happening so quickly,' he softened his voice, 'I didn't plan it. God knows I would never want to do anything to hurt you. It's just one of those things. We met at work and she—'

Barbara pulled her hand away, put her finger to her lips and shook her head. She read books for a living. She had skipped the first few chapters, but she knew how this story ended. She took her cup to the greenhouse and gave all her attention to her tomato plants, pinching outside shoots and tying in stems, wiping away washes of tears with her sleeves. She stayed there until she heard his car leaving.

Three weeks later, she was driving back from the solicitors, her marriage all but over. She had stayed standing during the meeting, refused tea and used her own pen. She wouldn't know how she felt for a long time. Turning on the radio to drown out the morning, she caught the end of her favourite song from her college days. She wished she could hear it from the start. Barbara had a habit of playing a song again and again until it keeled over. It drove her husband crazy. He would plead with her to play something new. 'But everything I need right now is in this song', she would explain. It was how she felt in her greenhouse, with potting compost under her fingernails and in her hair, searching for a packet of seeds that she just had in her hand, or finding shoots that had pushed their shoulders up through the dark overnight and were now lifting their heads to the light.

She parked her car but didn't bother going into the house. Straight through the side gate, stripping off her black, don't-mess-with-me jacket and flinging it on a bench. She pulled her earrings from her ears, kicked off her shoes and slid her feet into a pair of ugly rubber garden shoes that she would like to be buried in. Her tomato plants were now three feet high and covered in tiny yellow stars, but the leaves were drooping and the soil was dry. She started plant triage immediately and swore that nothing else would get in the way of their care.

The house sold without having a sign erected beside the front gate. She was thankful for that, but it meant that she only had a month to leave. Her husband was already holed up with the woman who made him feel young again, so he just wanted the cheque. He had also promised the children the panacea of a generous cash gift so lots of helpful pressure was applied to get Barbara out of the house, including a bargain bin mindfulness book entitled 'Moving on with Joy'. She mindfully shredded each page and sprinkled them on top of her grass clippings.

She found an apartment that she could just about afford. As she signed on the dotted line, she said a prayer that one of her authors would have a bestseller at some point before she died. She did not canvass anyone's views on the property and couldn't explain why she chose it. Nor would she share her new address widely until she was settled, fearing that a single New Home! greeting card would be enough to send her into a deep decline.

Barbara would not accept a suggested late May or early June deadline to leave the family home. Did these people know anything about how tomatoes actually grow? In the middle of June, she fielded phone calls from both her children. Clearly, they had held summit talks. Did they think she was holding out for a reconciliation? She walked out to the garden and balanced her phone on the edge of the compost heap so she could deadhead Rosa *'Graham Thomas'* while her son and then her daughter expressed empathy tinged with impatience. Barbara counted the wilted roses with each snip and made the occasional 'I'm listening' noise, eventually pressing the mute button and telling them exactly what to do with their concern.

Finally, it was Sunday, July 2nd. Friday had been her absolute deadline to leave the house, but summer heat had returned, and she needed another 48 hours. Her husband was in Greece so she had simply called the estate agent and said that she needed more time and if they wanted the house they would have to wait until after lunch on Sunday, and no, she wouldn't be answering her phone again.

She woke on the nose of 8am. The day broke quiet— so quiet—and warm. Wandering into the almost empty kitchen, she looked out and saw that the air vents had already opened in the roof of the greenhouse. That was a good sign, but she wouldn't go out yet. She made the last cup of tea she would ever drink in her house. Even with bare walls and most of the furniture gone, it felt like her home. The morning light cast the shape of a sail across the wood floor. By lunchtime it would move to where the table used to be, but by then it would be someone else's light. She drained her cup and got dressed.

She walked out to the greenhouse bringing a big colander and a pair of scissors. Pulling away the brick that held the door closed, she stepped inside, the air filled with the scent of warm, fuzzy tomato leaves—a musty, herby smell with touches of tobacco and lemons. Describing the smell of tomato plants reminded her of a wine tasting event she went to with her husband and how they had giggled every time someone swirled their glass and suggested *'Fresh tennis balls'*. Like bold kids swinging on their chairs and daring the teacher to kick them out. She leaned back against the potting bench and closed her eyes, committing to memory the feeling of glass-hot sun on her face.

Before the year was out, she would hear reports of her ex-husband's first 10K run. His new partner was a list of everything Barbara wasn't. It hurt like hell, but right now she was busy saving her summer. Her first tomato harvest would be her last. The *Indigo Rose* tomatoes were an extraordinary colour. Not quite black, but the darkest shiny purple you could imagine. Most of them had only started to colour but there was a group of three near the top that were as perfect as snooker balls. The *Sungold* cherry tomatoes hung in long bunches like extravagant Mardi Gras earrings, deep orange baubles at the top and fading to bright yellow and then lime green at the bottom. But the *Gardener's Delight* stole her heart, as they always did. Branches weighed down with deep red picture book tomatoes, every one as perfect as the last. She had an hour before the new owners arrived, so she worked her scissors until the colander was heaving. Then she dragged the pots outside, dumped the plants on the compost heap and walked away.

She placed the colander of tomatoes on the passenger seat, the ripest ones resting on top. Her laundry bag was in the footwell, and her hairbrush was in the cupholder. The boot and backseat were packed with all the stuff the movers didn't move. She left all of her big gardening tools behind, but still planned to arrive at friends' houses armed and dangerous with a secateurs and a pair of gardening gloves ready to put manners on an overgrown shrub. She patted the rim of the colander and drove like she was taking her first baby home from the hospital.

The apartment that was now her home had no balcony,

but the sun shone through the kitchenette window for a couple of hours each day, at least in summer. Barbara laid the green tomatoes along the windowsill to ripen in the company of a basil plant. She opened the first box labelled 'kitchen' and found a gold-rimmed soup bowl from her wedding china. Her first instinct was to fling it across the room with the force of an Olympic shot-put champion. But instead, she filled it with orange, purple and red tomatoes, still warm from the car and ready to burst.

Kicking off her sandals, she hiked herself up on the hot worktop, letting her feet rest in the sink. Barbara liked to know where she stood (or sat) in the world. Out the window, she could see in the distance the red and white striped chimneys of Dublin Port. That meant the Wicklow mountains were straight ahead of her and her greenhouse was behind. She unfolded a threadbare tea towel, laid it across her knees and let the juices fall.

Printed in Great Britain
by Amazon